The Christmas Mistake

The
Christmas
Mistake

Josephine Templeton

Praise be to God, Jesus, and the Holy Spirit!

To my honey, Mike - so thankful for the life God has blessed upon us.

A special thank you to Sunni Nichols for taking time to be this book's first reader!

Prologue

Hotel Monteleone – Room # 333

New Orleans, LA

Dec 24th, 2016

4:05 PM

Dressed only in matching Christmas-themed bra and underwear, Carina stared into blue eyes that should have been brown. "You're not my fiancé."

The handsome man took his time checking her out and whistled. "No...which is a shame."

Chapter 1

Hotel Monteleone - 3rd Floor Hallway

New Orleans, LA

Saturday, Dec 24th, 2016

4:00 PM

I can't believe I willingly put myself in an empty refrigerator box to surprise my fiancé for Christmas.

Carina sat on a suitcase with her hands clasped over her knees. Her thumbs tapped together nearly as fast as a hummingbird's wings. A thousand of those delicate birds played Frisbee in her stomach, and she regretted having pizza for lunch. The red sauce added spews of volcanic activity to the acidic contents of the birds' playground.

What am I doing…this is nuts. He's lost interest… maybe I have, too…four years is a long time to date someone…fresh out of college…too serious too soon …

This little escapade was completely out of her character. The idea of a surprise visit to her boyfriend had popped into her head while watching romantic Christmas movies. Loneliness had spurred her on, and after watching heroine after heroine break out of their shell in movie after movie, she garnered the courage to do the same.

Fear chewed at her brain. *What if…what if…he's asleep?*

Her thumbs increased their battle against each other, and her right eye twitched. *I should call this off. He won't be happy if I wake him up. But then again, he did ask me to be more spontaneous…*

2

Several weeks ago, Bart had woken her up by banging on her apartment door in the middle of the night. She had stumbled out of bed, shrugging into the robe that she kept handy for just such occasions. Her heartbeat had pounded in her ears like a tornado rushing over a town. She had rushed to open the door, fearful of whatever bad thing that had caused him to just show up and not call.

Upon opening the door, the alcohol on his breath had immediately infiltrated her nose, and she had been certain she would fail a Breathalyzer test just from the fumes coming out of his mouth. He had leaned against the door jam and leered at her boobs. He had reached for them, and she had deftly knocked his hand away.

"Gurl, ya need to be more spoonta…sponta…liciousness," he had slurred. Upon uttering the words, he rocked forward in an attempt to hug her. She had jumped back and watched him land in a heap at her feet. Crossing her arms, Carina stared at him as he started to snore.

'I haven't seen you in two weeks…supposedly 'cause you were working…and now you are passed out drunk on my floor…ON A TUESDAY night.' She had whispered the words, as though she had been relieved he had passed out. She had been exhausted from work and had no desire to babysit a drunk— one who seemed intent on pawing his way into her bed. Not happening, buddy.

Carina was jolted back in to the present when the box stopped moving. She adjusted her rump on the suitcase. She inhaled through her nose, filling her lungs as her yoga instructor had taught, and expelled the breath through her mouth.

3

I'm crazy. Her index finger made circles around her right temple. Nobody could see her. The gesture was meant to help distract herself...or not. *Why am I doing this? After that episode, I should be kicking him to the curb.*

The box tilted again, bringing her back to the present. Her hands flew out to steady herself and pressed against thin cardboard. Her fingers rubbed against one of the holes. Without them, she'd probably suffocate in the old box ingrained with the scent of must. The smart, young bellman had carved them out for her.

"Sorry, ma'am," he whispered.

"It's okay. I'm fine." She breathed in deep and exhaled slowly, recalling her earlier arrival.

Many hotels in the French Quarter of New Orleans offered this service. Parking lots were an option, but she hadn't wanted to drag her luggage down the uneven sidewalks and through the crowded streets.

Pulling the large Chevy truck into the nearest temporary slot, she had flung open the door, accidentally slamming it into the wall. Carina had shrugged. The truck was old and could take the abuse. Her Paw-Paw had left the ole girl to her, and even though it had been built in 1993, it ran as smooth as cat's gruff purr— deep and steady with a slight touch of hiccups. Sliding out, she made sure the oversized, black trench coat covered her down to her high heels. A cold breeze whipped through the parking garage and up her bare legs. She wore next to nothing, and she prayed the coat didn't magically pop open somehow. That would not only be cold but embarrassing. Her hand rested on the cold green metal, sending shivers over her skin. She pushed the creaky truck door shut, actually taking comfort in the sound of the squeaky hinges.

An older valet approached her wearing the hotel's standard black uniform with gold stripes on the wrists. He wore a black golf cap over his bald head, and his blue eyes held a twinkle that matched his smile.

"Merry Christmas, little lady."

"And a very Merry one to you." she smiled as she handed over her keys. He gave her a ticket and began helping her unload her stuff onto the cart. The suitcase fit well, but the Christmas wrapped refrigerator box battled with the bars on the cart. The old fellow raised his left eyebrow but said nothing. She was a grateful for that.

"I have a dolly." Carina pulled it out of the bed. "Let's put the suitcase inside."

Once they got everything situated, she tipped him before he pushed the dolly to a red-haired young man waiting by the hotel door. He jumped into action and pushed the dolly into the hotel. Before they got too far inside, Carina put her hand on his shoulder.

"Excuse me." Her heart fluttered nervously. Actually putting her request into words sent anxiety flying through her. She took a deep breath. "I need a huge favor from you."

He stopped, turned his head in her direction, and narrowed his eyes. "Lady, you're a looker fer sure, but I don't do funny stuff."

Her stunted laugh echoed in the confined hallway. She waved her hand. "No, no, nothing like that. I just need … well, my fiancé is here, and I'm his Christmas present. So, I just need a hand getting

5

into the box. I'll give you two hundred bucks to deliver me to his room."

The young man's facial features relaxed, and he nodded his head. "Oh. Yeah. No problem. Let's go to the luggage holding room."

"Can I just jump in the box here? I'd rather not risk running into him before the big surprise." Carina shifted from foot to foot, hoping that her fiancé wouldn't suddenly appear before them.

The hotel was pretty busy, and people rushed around them constantly. Many automatically moved around like salmon avoiding rocks as they swam upstream. Others glared at her and the bellhop, mumbling under their breath as they passed. She avoided eye contact with them, hoping nobody guessed that she only wore underwear beneath the trench coat.

Louisiana at Christmas could be warm enough to wear shorts. She thanked the Heavens that a cold front had blown in that morning. While the people of New Orleans were used to seeing all manners of dressed or undressed individuals, Carina's conservative style made her super self-conscious. Add that to her current state of nervousness, and she would have tripped over everything in sight or knocked it over. She tended to become a klutz during such times.

The bellhop ran a hand through his red hair. He twisted his head around, surveying the passing guests and shrugged. "Sure, but let's get out of the way."

After moving the dolly to an area out of the way of other hotel guests, he peered inside the box. Taking out a pocketknife, he poked some holes in the side. "Wouldn't want you to suffocate."

"Thanks," Carina smiled. She handed him the cash and a slip of paper with the room number on it. "Hopefully, I won't be in there that long."

Once she got inside, the bellman closed the makeshift door and taped it up. "It's a shame you won't see our lobby. The decorations are very pretty. Want me to cut a tiny hole in the door so you can see?"

"As long as it's not noticeable, sure." The inside of the box was darker than a bayou in the middle of night, so a little light would be comforting. Carina slipped off the trench coat and pulled a silk robe out of the pocket. She let the coat fall to her feet, and she sat on the suitcase and placed her stiletto's on top of the coat. She twisted the silk robe between her hands, letting the softness calm her bundle of nerves. She hoped everything continued going smoothly.

Seconds later, a hole the size of her pinky let in light. The box rocked as the bellman tipped the dolly. He rolled her through the hotel. She peeked through the hole, and the sight of the Christmas trees lining the halls lightened her heart. She loved this holiday the best, and with happy thoughts of surprising her fiancé, she hummed one of her favorite songs: "It's Beginning to Look A lot like Christmas."

Chapter 2

Hotel Monteleone - 3rd Floor Hallway

New Orleans, LA

Saturday, Dec 24ᵗʰ, 2016

4:00 PM

It's beginning to look a lot like Christmas…everywhere I go…

Carina sang the lyrics in her head and hummed the tune low. Anything to distract her from the nerves working on her resolve. She was going to go through with this and be spontaneous. She ignored the doubts beating at her brain; it was too late for what-if's. She'd spent way too much time and money setting this up.

Just got to get through this first part…then we can go have some dinner and enjoy Christmas in the French Quarter.

A ding echoed outside of the box, indicating the elevator had reached a floor. The heavy doors whooshed open. The young bellman coughed and grunted as he pushed the box. The dolly wheels rolled over the elevator door, and the box teetered precariously. He groaned, and there was a touchy moment when Carina's world tilted too much to one side. Her hands instantly flattened against the sides of the box as she stifled a yelp. Her heart had already been thrumming in her ears like hummingbird wings, but this pushed her heart into the roar of a jet passing too close overhead.

"Hey, remember I'm in here."

"Sorry, miss," the young man whispered.

The box retained its warmth, especially now as her body heat revved up from the scare. Despite that, her teeth chattered, obviously from nerves. She forced her hands back around her knees, letting her thumbs resume tapping against one another.

What if Bart gets mad?

"Stop it, Carina," she muttered under her breath. Time for a new beginning. Things in the past should stay there. Bart had promised never to…

She shook her head, refusing to dwell. *Happy, happy, happy…this WILL be fun.* Her trench coat as well as her silk red robe lay pooled at her feet, and she adjusted the strap of her Christmas bikini top. She had stayed covered while the bellhop closed her up in the box. Her current attire was for one pair of eyes only. Since her fiancé couldn't be home for the Christmas holidays, she had decided to bring the festivities to Bart. His business trip was in New Orleans, and as Baton Rouge was only an hour away, she'd figured what the Christmas bells.

It's been awhile since…well, I sure hope this spices things up enough for him.

A few minutes later, the box jolted to a stop, and a muffled knock filtered through the box. She couldn't see the bellhop, but she envisioned him tapping on the hotel room door. Her heart continued racing like a Christmas mouse running from a cat. Door locks clicked, and hinges squeaked. She attempted to make out the muffled voices. When the box jolted into movement, she struggled not to panic at the odd sensation. It was hard enough not to freak about the moment Bart opened his present.

The door shut, and heavy footsteps crossed the floor and up to the box. Silence beat against her ears, and she held her breath. The anticipation made her want to kick open the cardboard door and dance out into Bart's astonished but grateful arms. She imagined the delight in his eyes, like it was when they first began dating.

Carina tensed as the wrapping paper ripped. She straightened the Santa hat on her head before placing her hands on her knees. Pulling back her shoulders, she thrust out her chest. The mistletoe around her neck itched, but she resisted the urge to scratch. A nervous smile threatened to turn into jittery giggles.

The makeshift door carved into the box swung open, and Carina squinted at the bright light. She assumed it came from the bathroom as she was temporarily blinded. More silence bounced off the walls, broken only by a low, sexy whistle.

"Well, I guess I've been a very, very good boy," drawled an unfamiliar voice.

She blinked several times, and as her eyes adjusted, her mouth fell open. She stared into blue eyes that should have been brown. Her heart froze, despite the red fire crawling up her neck. The bellhop had delivered her to the wrong room.

So much for the kid being smart.

The man's gaze travelled from her face, over her bosom, and down to her stilettos. His half-grin unexpectedly melted her mistletoe. His muscular bare chest had a light dusting of curly hair that tapered down into red Christmas boxers with candy canes all over them…and matched her bikini exactly. For a brief second, she appreciated his well-toned body. Then she came to her wits.

She had several options: freak out and run screaming from the room, play it cool and slip out of the room without a word, or chose option three.

"Eeeep," she said, emulating a buzzer on a game show. "Wrong. You've been naughty, not nice, and Santa has just played a cruel trick on you."

Heart hammering in her throat, Carina slipped off the suitcase. She tried to slide past him to the door, but his warm fingers wrapped around her bare arm. Yet instead of feeling threatened, the touch sent interesting vibes over her skin.

"Whoa there," he drawled. "Where d'ya think you're going?"

As the heat sizzled up her arm, she sucked in her breath, fighting the instant attraction. She was engaged and here to see her fiancé, not to have a one-night stand with a complete stranger … albeit an incredibly handsome one.

"This"— she yanked her arm free and pointed at her bikini— "is meant for someone else. Merry Christmas, dude, but I'm outta here."

He stepped in front of her with his hands up, and the bathroom light played over his face. He shook his sandy colored bangs out of his eyes. "Don't take this the wrong way, but you're half-naked. Should you be running down the hall in a New Orleans hotel like that?"

Carina glanced at her skimpy outfit, and her cheeks heated. *Thank the Lord I hadn't accidentally run into Maw-Maw.* Then again, what would the recently widowed lady be doing down in New Orleans

11

instead of safe in her Baton Rouge home? Maw-Maw hated Louisiana's City of Sin.

But there would be people roaming the hotel corridors at this time of night who were probably drunk. Unfortunately, they would also be disorderly, and she had no desire to deal with alcohol drenched, would-be Romeos…or even Juliet's.

"It's all right. I have this to cover up with, so it's all good." Backing up, she knelt beside the refrigerator box, grabbed the red silk robe, and stood at the same time. The material caught on the suitcase and yanked her off balance. She teetered on her heels but managed to stay on her feet and keep ahold of the robe. Her cheeks flamed with more embarrassing heat, but she pulled her shoulders back and slipped on the robe.

The guy crossed his arms and whistled low. "You still look hot as a firecracker."

"Thanks, but like I said earlier, this was a mistake. Now if you'll excuse me, I have to go find my fiancé." Carina slipped her hands in the pockets of the robe, and her fingers clasped around her car key. She could use it in defending herself should this dude try anything funny.

"Do you think you could at least help me clean up this mess?" He pointed to the wrapping paper strewn about the floor.

Carina glanced over the room, taking in the total disarray from the unmade beds to food wrappers covering the dresser. She rolled her eyes. "'Cause it will clearly make a difference."

"Well, I'm not talking about the entire room." The light from the bathroom shone on his face, and the corners of his mouth lifted while his blues eyes sparkled, a clear indication that he found the situation amusing.

"Nobody told you to rip the paper to shreds," she grumbled. Her already racked nerves escalated, and her teeth ground against each other. She forced herself to relax her jaw, but her hands remained balled into fists.

"Nobody told you to deliver yourself to my room." The dude sparred words with her, and he seemed to be enjoying himself. "Even though I'm glad you were."

She narrowed her eyes, unsure of where this was headed. Backing up, she quickly began picking up paper, surprised when he helped her. He moved the suitcase and picked up her cell phone, setting it on the dresser.

A few minutes later, they had everything picked up with the box torn down. Once it was all in the hall, he stood in the doorway, waiting.

"Well," Carina held out her hand. "Nice to meet you."

He slipped his hand in hers, and the warmth permeated her skin. His eyes twinkled. "It was incredibly nice to see you again."

Chapter 3

Hotel Monteleone – Rad's hotel room # 333

New Orleans, LA

Saturday, Dec 24ᵗʰ, 2016

4:00 PM

Rad stepped out of the shower and grabbed the last clean towel from the metal shelf above the toilet. He patted his body completely dry before slipping on a pair of red boxers decorated with Christmas candy canes. He shook his head, wondering why he had kept the gift from his recently-caught-cheating-ex-girlfriend.

"Battle-ax," he whispered. He said it louder a few more times, trying to get it out of his system. Didn't work.

"Have a holly jolly Christmas," sang Alan Jackson. The song played on the television's music station. Rad sang along as he left the bathroom, and his left foot crushed a pizza box. Snarling, he shook his head.

"I so regret the Do Not Disturb sign," he mumbled to the empty room.

Last night's pizza party had started off the evening, and after carousing the streets of the French Quarter, the party ended back here at around three am. He barely remembered climbing into bed, but he vividly recalled the ice water hitting his chest. He had jumped up hollering, ready to bust the nearest culprit in the mouth. His buddies, Chip, Darren, and Sean laughed at him from across the room, but they calmed him down by promising him a juicy hamburger for lunch. They'd hit the streets at about noon, back on the prowl.

This weekend was a guy's only trip. Yet his buddies had ditched him for out-of-town college girls. *Traitors.* They had tried to get him to hook up with one of the girls, but when they weren't paying attention, he had slipped into the crowd. They'd been too drunk to notice, and by the time they did, they were too wasted to care.

Rad had no desire for a one-night stand or even a new long-term stand. Despite his recent social media status change from *in-a-relationship* to *single*, he needed a break from women in general. Funny thing about it was that even though it was the holidays, he was more relieved than sad. Why does society pressure people so much to be in a relationship? Why does the vast majority believe that one must be with someone in order to be happy? He wanted to focus on himself, be selfish, and check off items on his bucket list before tying himself down to another woman.

Towel drying his hair, he sat on the bed. Yes, he wanted a family, but right now, his parents needed him. He was the youngest of five kids, but the other siblings lived out of state. He lived next door to his folks just to really be there for them.

Shaking his head, he noticed his phone blinked with a message. He picked it up, confirming it was from one of his buds, Chip. *Where y'at? We found ya a hottie.*

He tossed the phone on the bed, ignoring the text. When he had slipped away from them earlier, he had hoped they would forget about him for a while. He had no interest in fooling around with

15

under-aged women. There was no way those girls were of age despite the game of dress up they played. High heels, short skirts, and too much makeup only made them appear silly to him. They had squealed too much and jittered nervously despite their attempt to appear cool with the New Orleans scene. *Fish out of water.* They were probably Catholic high school girls on a sneak out.

To be quite honest, he preferred the artistic side of New Orleans versus the party life. He enjoyed hunting down antiques in the French Quarter for his shop in Baton Rouge, and sometimes, he acquired art from the street vendors to resell. He believed in supporting starving artists instead of feeding the corporate piggy bank. He had secretly hoped to do more of that this weekend than drinking it up. That ship, however, had sailed.

His cell phone played *You're a Mean One, Mr. Grinch.* In his brain, he always heard Mrs. Grinch. His heart dropped at the thought of his ex. *What the devil did she want now?*

Snatching his phone off the dresser, he sat on the edge of the messed-up bed, wrinkling his nose at the smell of spilled beer. The spot on the floor had dried, but that combined with the dozen or so empty bottles kept the room smelling like a bar. He wished again that he had not put out the Do Not Disturb sign. The place was in desperate need of a cleaning lady.

Scrolling through his ex's mile long text, the words listing her items left at his house blurred. He responded with *whatever* and tossed the phone back on the dresser. He considered blocking her number and didn't fight the memory of their parting of the ways. *Had it only been three weeks ago?*

16

They had been at her work's Christmas party. She had gone to the restroom, and thirty minutes later, Rad had gone to check on her. The night's festivities were winding down, and only a handful of people remained. It had been time to leave, and he feared she'd passed out in the bathroom. She'd started tossing them back before they left the house, so he knew he was the designated driver for the evening. Once they'd gotten there, she had headed to the bar for more.

Two ladies exited the bathroom, and he had asked if they had seen her. The women had glanced at each other before both vehemently insisting nobody was in there. He instantly became suspicious and rushed past them. Entering the ladies' room, he froze at the sound of lips smacking in what was an obvious make out session. He pushed open the door on every stall until revealing his fiancé and another woman.

Instead of feeling sad, a huge weight had lifted off Rad's shoulders. For some reason, he hadn't been surprised, and even now, his eyes remained dry. Everything had fallen into place like the pieces of a puzzle. The late-night calls and weekend sleepovers she had spent with her girlfriend. It now seemed a more than appropriate word for the bestie who always hung around.

Now I know why.

A tap on the hotel door shook him out of the stinging memory. The knock turned into two more forceful and solid blows. Rad's brow furrowed.

Better not be one my idiot friends trying to drag me back out, he thought sourly. Not happening.

17

Reluctance coursed through him as he dragged himself off the bed and over to the door. He peered through the peephole but only saw something bright red that blocked his view. Grunting in exasperation, Rad's hand flipped away the lock and wrapped around the door handle. Hesitating, he considered ignoring the knock. Whatever his friends had planned, it did not bode well. However, he knew how persistent they could be. They'd never stop knocking, so he opened the door, fully prepared to argue with several drunks.

A bellman stood next to a box the size of a refrigerator wrapped in red Christmas paper. The pimple faced fellow shifted from one foot to another, as if he'd rather have been elsewhere. He tugged on the sleeves of his black coat. The hotel's gold emblem was embroidered on the breast pocket, and a pair of black glasses poked out of it.

Rad's eyes narrowed as suspicion clouded his brain. He peered up and down the hall before pointing the box. "What's this?"

The young man's face remained bright red. He shrugged and refused to look Rad in the eye. "Dunno. Was just asked to bring it to your room. I gotta get back downstairs, so if you step aside, I'll get it in your room."

Warning bells clanged in his head, but Rad stepped aside and let the bellman and huge box inside. He watched the man struggle with the oversized object, but certain it was all just a prank anyway, he crossed his arms and refused to help. There was a moment of awkwardness after the box was situated. Rad just looked at the bellman. He was sure his buddies had paid the guy well for his services, so he wasn't about to tip him. The guy quickly realized that and made a hasty exit, leaving Rad alone in the hotel room with the mysterious box.

Those damn drunk idiots better not have sent me what I think this is. Or rather, who…

With the tip of his index finger, Rad tore a strip of paper off the box. Before long, paper fluttered to the floor, and a refrigerator box stood before him. A makeshift door had been carved into the box, and he pulled it open.

It was as he expected— a woman. But not the one he expected…or type. The brunette before him exuded elegance— from the high curve of her cheekbone to the designer Christmas lingerie that matched his own. He'd bet money she wasn't a prostitute, and if she wasn't, then what the hell was she doing in his hotel room?

Dressed only in matching Christmas-themed bra and underwear, the woman stared into his eyes. Her mouth fell open in a soft, round shape.

"You're not my fiancé."

Rad took his time checking her out and whistled. "No…which is a shame."

Chapter 4

Hotel Monteleone — Rad's hotel room # 333

New Orleans, LA

Saturday, Dec 24th, 2016

4:05 PM

The woman squinted at Rad from her perch on a suitcase, but he made no move to block the light pouring from the bathroom. His mouth watered at the lovely legs perched awkwardly atop a bundled up black coat. Her hands remained folded over her knees, and the red nail polished blended nicely with her creamy skin. A low whistle escaped his lips before he had time to even think *sexual harassment.*

Well, it's a tad late to try claiming that in the future...seeing as how this little lady appeared in MY hotel room...in her underwear, to boot. So, let's have a little fun...

"Well, I guess I've been a very, very good boy," he drawled, taking a step back into an admiring pose complete with crossed arms and his right hand rubbing his chin thoughtfully. He deliberately enhanced his southern accent. If he was going to toy with this lady, he had to lay it on thick. Not that he would brag, but he did get hit on by women of all ages. So, by now, he knew what worked best for him. He tried to refrain from cutesy pickup lines that his buds forever dropped on women.

He loved how her eyelashes fluttered, and her pink lips parted into an o-shape the size of a peppermint candy. Something familiar about her gnawed at the back of his brain, but his libido had gone

20

into overtime. The game of cat and mouse had begun, and he had every intention of completing the pass. If his buddies had set him up with this hottie, then maybe he *should* accept the much-needed distraction. Everyone needed a rebound fling, didn't they?

He allowed his gaze to travel from her face, over her bosom, and down to her stilettos. Even though he toyed with her, heat filled him, and he shifted to hide his interest. Her matching Christmas underwear left little to the imagination, and he forced himself to think of pouring a pitcher of ice down his boxers. No need to blow the game by overshooting the pass.

"Eeeep," she said, emulating a buzzer on a game show. Her arms crossed over her chest, in a feeble attempt to hide the soft mounds peeping out of the candy-cane covered bra. "Wrong. You've been naughty, not nice, and Santa just played a cruel trick on you."

The woman uncrossed her legs, slipped off the suitcase and tried to slide past him. He slipped his fingers around her bare arm, and her smooth skin sent sensuous, electric shocks down to the area he just poured imaginary ice over.

*Snow…snow…snow…*Hard to imagine snow down in the south, but Rad did everything in his power to hide his definite interest from the woman. Hopefully, the candy canes on his boxers helped. He shifted, hoping nothing poked out in an obvious manner.

"Whoa there," he drawled. "Where d'ya think you're going?"

She froze, sucking in her breath. She lifted her chin high and straightened her back. Rad braced himself for a good solid tongue lashing. *Oh Lord, I've done woken a hornet's nest.*

21

"This"— she yanked free her arm free and pointed at her bikini— "is meant for someone else. Merry Christmas, dude, but I'm outta here."

Rad's brows furrowed, and a touch of disappointment entered his mood. So, this wasn't set up by those idiots. Shouldn't be surprised…those dummies were too drunk by now to set up a stunt like this. Too bad…She definitely would have been an amazing gift from Santa.

His gentleman upbringing rose to the surface, and he stepped in front of her with his hands up, shaking his bangs out of his eyes. "Don't take this the wrong way, but you're half naked. Should you be running down the hall in a New Orleans hotel like that?"

As the woman glanced at her outfit, he could almost see the light bulb go off in her brain. Her cheeks flushed from a light pink to a blazing bright red. "It's all right. I have this to cover up with, so it's all good."

She turned, and the bathroom light fell on the curve of her behind. Rad stared some more, unable to keep his thoughts from going to that place of sweet cotton candy and Christmas bliss. When she bent to reach inside the refrigerator box, her rump lifted, and his eyes widened. All traces of alcohol left his body in favor of his libido, and his hands instantly covered the tell-tale sign of his attraction to this woman. He desperately wished he had a pillow close by, but any movement might reveal his own candy cane to her. So, he stood rooted to the spot, envisioning jumping into a pool filled with ice cubes.

The woman grabbed the red silk robe and stood at the same time. The material caught on the suitcase and yanked her off balance.

She teetered on her heels but managed to stay on her feet and keep ahold of the robe. Biting her lower lip, she pulled her shoulders back and slipped on the robe. The bathroom light bounced against her soft mounds before she pulled the robe tight and cinched the silky belt around her curvy waist.

Distracted by the flesh before him, Rad simply stared as his mouth watered. Licking his lips, he briefly closed his eyes and took a calming breath. *Down, boy, down…*

Opening his eyes, he crossed his arms and wiggled his eyebrows. "You still look hot as a firecracker."

"Thanks, but like I said earlier, this was a mistake. Now, if you'll excuse me, I have to go find my fiancé." She slipped her hands in the robe's pockets.

"Do you think you could at least help me clean up this mess?" Still unable to move his hands, he nodded toward the wrapping paper all over the floor.

With her nose raised, she surveyed the room, clearly taking note of the horrible mess. She faced him, put her hands on her hips and rolled her eyes. "'Cause it will clearly make a difference."

"Well, I'm not talking about the entire room."

"Nobody told you to rip the paper to shreds," she grumbled.

"Nobody told you to deliver yourself to my room," Rad snapped. He heard the snip in his words and hastened to soften the blow. "Even though I'm glad you were."

She glared at him through narrowed eyes, and when her hands dropped from her waist, he knew he'd won the battle. Backing up, she quickly began picking up paper, and Rad took that moment

23

to grab the hotel robe from the closet. Then, he took to dissembling the cardboard box, the bottom of which was a wooden crate.

Smart woman.

Had it just been the cardboard beneath her, she probably would have fallen through the box, despite the dolly beneath. He wondered what had given her the idea and hoped the fiancé deserved and appreciated her.

Country Christmas music filled the sudden silence, and he found himself humming along. While they worked, his mind spun, trying to grasp why she seemed so familiar. As she bent down to pick up her suitcase, the back of her neck stretched enticingly. It also revealed a tiny cat tattoo beneath her left ear. Underneath the black feline was one word written in cursive: *Foxie*.

The memory of who she was crashed into him like a Christmas tree falling out of the back of a pickup truck. His heart hammered in his chest, and his palms began to sweat. How in the world could he *not* have recognized her? He subtly studied for signs of the girl he had once known.

Heck, he had been with her the day she had gotten that tattoo. It had been done out of love for a recently deceased feline. The sweet, old creature had been a part of her life since birth. In fact, the kitty had been born on the same day and found by her dad on a smoke break while at the hospital. Of course, he also remembered that the tattoo was part of a rebellion against her father, who, at the time, had been forcing her to go to some hoity-toity college to become a nurse. By the look of things, Rad assumed that's what happened.

In short order, they had everything picked up with the box torn down. Once it was all in the hall, he stood in the doorway, waiting.

"Well," she held out her hand. "Nice to meet you."

He slipped his hand in hers, and the warmth permeated her skin. His eyes twinkled, and he wondered if, by some small chance, she even recognized a trace of the high school boy he used to be. A lazy smile drifted over his face. "It was incredibly nice to see you again."

Chapter 5

Hotel Monteleone - Rad's hotel room # 333

New Orleans, LA

Saturday, December 24th, 2016

4:35 PM

Carina stared at the man's fingers holding her hand. The warmth from his skin seeped into her own, and his touch sent waves of heat through her. She froze like a fawn under the gaze of a hunter, lost in a spell. *What would it be like to be loved by this man? His hands are so gentle yet firm…unlike Bart's sweaty palms.*

Her cheeks became firey from embarrassment, as if she had just eaten hot sauce, and her stomach churned as if filled with too much spice from a crawfish boil. Her soul cringed with guilt. Even though she hadn't physically done anything to resemble cheating on Bart, her thoughts were definitely going someplace they had no right to be. *Carina, shame on you. Just because it's been awhile between you and Bart…*

The man's thumb rubbed over bruises on her wrist. She cringed, hoping he wouldn't realize they were shaped like fingers. An image of her fiancé screaming at her slammed into her mind. He had left on this trip straight after their fight, and she hoped to patch things up now. Nobody should fight on Christmas, even though they do.

"Frankly, my dear"— Carina's cellphone vibrated on the dresser— "tomorrow is another day."

The phone repeated the snippets from *Gone with the Wind*, her aunt's favorite movie. It drowned out the Christmas music playing on the TV. Sanity rushed back with sudden clarity, and her cheeks flamed with embarrassment. She wrenched her hand free and took a step toward the room.

"That's my cell phone," she murmured as he allowed her to rush past him. She was too late, though, and missed the call. As she turned back to leave, her heel caught on a piece of the box which they had somehow missed while cleaning up. She danced backward, trying to remain upright and fell against the dresser. Her hand landed in a bowl of ice-cold nacho cheese, and with a soft cry, she jumped back, slinging it everywhere.

Carina collided against a hard, male chest, and the stranger's arms kept her from falling on the floor. His embrace became cozy, reminding her of campfire dates and happier times. *What an odd thought* ... She squirmed out of his arms, and this time, her butt ended up in the cheese bowl.

"Oh, crud! I am such a ditz!" She slapped her hand to her forehead, smearing cheese over her face. The cold gooey mess slid down her nose.

When she realized what she'd done, her eyes widened, and her mouth formed an o-shape. It was hard not to see the laughter in his eyes, and when deep chuckles erupted from him, they were contagious. Her mortification turned to mirth, and they both laughed for several minutes.

When they both stopped to catch their breath, moans came from the other side of the wall with an occasional man's voicing crying out, *"Thank you, Deirdra, spank me again."* The couple in the room over was getting busy, and the woman screamed, "Superman me, baby!"

Carina met the stranger's eyes, and they busted out laughing again. Once that session died down, the man held out his hand. "Rad LeBlanc."

She eyed his hand warily but placed her non-cheesy hand in his. "Carina de Brock."

Rad smiled and pulled her to the bathroom. "Go clean up."

"Thanks," she mumbled and started to close the door.

"Wait." Rad eased out of the hotel robe and handed it to her.

He now remained only in his Christmas boxers, which Carina refused to look at for fear of more unwanted thoughts. However, his attractive chest became a feast for her eyes. Golden hair dappled his masculine chest, just enough to make it fun for fingers to play with. His toned biceps confirmed the strength she had felt when he caught her a few minutes ago, and something inside her perked up with curiosity that she hadn't felt in a good while.

Accepting the garment, she smiled at him and shut the door. She faced the mirror and shook her head at the brunette staring back at her. "Way to go, goofball."

Grabbing a clean washcloth from the rack, she turned on the hot water and cleaned the gooey cheese off her face. She took off her makeup in the process and regretted leaving her overnight bag in the car.

Oh, well. Bart will have to get over it.

She doubted he would. The man was very adamant about her appearance. Sometimes she felt like a Stepford wife— er— fiancé, but his job demanded keeping up with the Jones'. So, she appeased his wishes and always managed to look her best every time she left the house.

Her cell phone dinged, and an image of her aunt popped up on the screen, followed by an incoming message from her aunt. *Rina, did you make it to the hotel yet?*

Aunt Mary had chestnut hair that was cut just above her shoulders, and she wore trendy brown glasses with white polka dots. Her mother's sister had taken over as a mother figure to Carina years ago, and the two were thick as thieves. Her mother's death four years ago…She shook herself, refusing to go down that road.

Picking up the cell, she typed a response. I made it fine, Mere-mere. Enjoy your own date, and stop worrying about me. Will see you soon, Auntie. Love you and Merry Christmas!

In the pocket of the red robe was a piece of cinnamon gum she'd put there earlier. She retrieved it and popped it in her mouth. She removed the cheese-covered, red robe and donned the plush hotel robe. Posing with pouty lips, she studied herself in the mirror, then laughed with a headshake.

Sexy and terrycloth do not go well together.

Opening the door, she stepped out into the room. Rad sat at the room's table, which was the size of a TV tray. He'd been staring at his cell but set it down to look at her.

Ah, he chose me over the phone. Nice change.

Carina dipped her chin to her chest and batted her eyes. She twirled around as if on the catwalk. "Definitely vogue-worthy, dontcha think?"

"Honey," he drawled. "You'd be hot in curlers and a mud-facial. Ain't no hiding that. Your fella...he's a lucky man, and I sure hope he appreciates you."

His smoldering gaze sent flames over her insides. She froze as an electric sexual tension filled the room. A huge chunk of her wanted to throw caution in the trashcan with the wrapping paper left over from Christmas morning. For the briefest of moments, she envisioned stalking over to him, pulling open the robe, and...

Holy mistletoe, what is wrong with me? No, I refuse to be attracted to a man other than my fiancé. Granted, said fiancé has been lacking in attention toward me, but fiancé, nonetheless. Of course, no wedding date has yet to be set despite Bart's proposal over a year ago ...

Her senses pounded her crazy thoughts like crushed candy canes on a Gingerbread House. She forced her gaze away, and she edged toward the door leading to the hallway. Her cell phone felt heavy in her hands, and she tucked it into the hotel robe's pocket.

"Well," she paused with a mini, nervous laugh. "It's late, and I'd still like to surprise my fiancé. Thanks for being such a sport about my mistake."

Rad jumped up, and the chair fell over in a rush. He hastily closed the distance between them. Every movement he made, however rushed it was, reminded her of a man-eating tiger, sizing up its prey. *Woman-eating tiger might be a better word.*

Afraid of what might happen if he touched her, she jerked open the door and stepped out just as he grabbed it. Holding it open, he continued to eat her up with his eyes. "I'm just sorry I wasn't your fiancé."

She gulped, wondering what life would be like with him as a boyfriend. He seemed spicy enough, but would his current sweetness remain? Or would he turn into a vicious tiger and tear her inside and out like her current fiancé?

Seriously, Carina, stop flirting with danger. And give Bart another chance. He's just stressed with all his work.

As Rad slowly pushed the door shut, their eyes never left each other until the door blocked the way. She continued to stare at the white wood and brass numbers, wondering if he remained on the other side. She started to press her fingers against the door, but the thought of him staring at her through the peephole made her self-conscious.

Come on, girl, you have a boyfriend to surprise. Shake a candy cane.

Chapter 6

Hotel Monteleone - Room 335

New Orleans, LA

Saturday, December 24th, 2016

4:50 PM

Carina glanced at the brass door numbers on the room she'd just left. The bellman had delivered her to room three-three-three, but it should have been three-three-five. A simple mistake as they were side-by-side. The odd rooms ran down one side and evens on the other.

Since the moaners were in the one to her right, she went to the one on her left. The number was three-three-one, and she frowned back in the direction of room three-three-three. Her stomach flipped, and her feet tried to remain glued to the carpet. She forced herself to retrace her steps and went past Rad's room.

The superman's room was three-three-five. The super-couple who were having an intense evening of so-called intimacy. Although, it seemed more like an evening in a circus tent. Carina imagined a trapeze bar-swing attached to the hotel room's ceiling with a naked man swinging upside down. She cringed at the thought of his elephant nose tossing about wildly.

That would hurt. Carina snorted. Besides, the word intimate is definitely too tame for what they were doing.

She clung to the belief that she did not know superman, despite the ball of acid settling in her stomach. She rolled her shoulders and tried to clear her mind. Besides, there wasn't room in the hotel for such contraptions…unless they had rooms specifically designed for such occasions. Stranger things have happened in New Orleans.

"I must have written down the wrong number," Carina mumbled under her breath.

She nibbled on her lower lip, crossed her arms and stared at the door, gathering up the courage to knock. Where she had been excited and full of nervous giggles only a short time before, now she wasn't so sure this had been one of her best ideas. In fact, the way things had started off, Fate had already hinted that she was in for a bumpy ride.

"Here we go," she whispered and rapped her knuckles against the cream-colored wood. She rubbed the engagement ring on her left hand as a heaviness settled in the pit of her stomach. What once seemed like a perfect idea was quickly escalating into a huge Christmas mistake.

A few long minutes later, the door creaked opened to reveal a scantily clad woman with disheveled red hair. The black bra barely covered her boobs, and the strip of black material covering her lower region left nothing to the imagination. Her lipstick smeared from her lips to her chin, and her green eye shadow had taken a wavy trip down her cheek. Her skin, especially her neck, was blotched red. Carina assumed from kisses. There was a huge hickey on her throat as well.

"What?" growled the red head. Her heeled toe tapped against the carpet. *Thump-thump-thump.* Like a rabbit who was late for a date.

Carina tried to see past the woman into the darkened room. A powerful perfume emanated from the woman. The musk tickled her nose, and she fought back a sneeze. Bart would never give the time of day to a woman who wore this cheap, heavy cologne. "Obviously I made a mistake. This has to be the wrong room."

"OMG," the woman whispered. Her brown eyes widened as if a speeding car was headed straight at her. Her attitude flipped from bossy to freaked out. "You're her."

The two women froze, assessing each other. The redhead backed up a couple steps and attempted to shut the door, but Carina flung her hip against the wood, pushing the other woman off balance. However, she remained close enough to the door to keep the room blocked from view. She stood a good two inches taller than Carina, so the blockage wasn't hard to accomplish.

Carina narrowed her eyes as her heart panged painfully. "Tell him to get his ass out here now."

The woman looked back over her shoulder and then back at Carina. "That might be hard to do at the moment ..."

Taking a short, deep breath, Carina placed her hands on the door and forced it open. She stepped on the woman's toes, and when the wench yelped in pain, Carina took the opportunity to push her way into the room. With her head held high, she strode in with the power of a woman scorned. The sight on the bed stopped her cold.

Her fiancé lay stretched out on the bed with his hands and legs cuffed to it. A mask covered his eyes and a gag over his mouth. But what caught her eye the most was the woman's Christmas pasties and the matching underwear he wore.

34

"Oh…my…God, Bart." Carina said each word slowly. Hysteria gathered in her chest, brewing up for the perfect Hurricane Carina. "You look ridiculous."

Nervous laughter bubbled up out of her throat and filled the room. The bizarre situation reminded her of a dark romantic comedy. The humor faded as the reality of the situation sank in.

Carina glared at the woman still standing by the open door. Her black latex bra and panty set screamed S&M. A black paddle the size of tennis racket sat loosely in her left hand. Clearly, she was his dominatrix.

Bart hollered, but the gag muffled it. The headboard rattled as he tried to jerk his arms free. His legs bounced against the mattress, but all that managed to do was shake the bed.

Carina pointed a finger at the woman. She wanted to rip the paddle from her and slam it over her head. "Set him free now, or I will rip your hair out."

The tone of her voice sent the woman scurrying to do just that. The redhead sat next to him and pulled off the blindfold. She pushed the gag down and touched his cheek with the paddle. "What is the safe word?"

Carina crossed her arms and tapped her foot. Bart glared at her from the bed. She chewed rapidly on the piece of gum.

"Carina." Bart spit the word out. His mouth clamped shut, and his thin face showed his jawline clearly. A muscle jumped in his cheek.

The redhead's shoulders relaxed, and she immediately undid his bonds. Bart sat up, pulling the covers over him. "Why the hell are you here?"

Carina cringed, but she was not backing down. No more. She was too strong to let him scare her into submission. Perhaps he had known that, and that's why he had resorted to his weekend escapades in New Orleans. He'd only hit her once, well, before the current bruises on her wrist. She had broken up with him, but he had crawled back with roses and wine and sparkling jewelry. He had never hit her again, but his words continued to bite just as deep if not deeper.

She drew herself up as tall as she could and held her head high. She peered down her nose at him. "To surprise you."

"Well, congrats. Job well done," he sneered. He stood, holding the bedcover tightly around him. "You never listen to me, Carina. I told you I'd be home tomorrow. Why the hell couldn't you have waited? Damn it. Now you've ruined everything. I hired her to teach me things so on our wedding night, I could in turn teach you."

Her mouth fell open, and her stomach bubbled like a Christmas apple pie, fresh out of the oven. The lies spewing from his mouth were unbelievable. "As if I'd ever…you…you lying piece of…of…shit!"

Bart's brown eyes darkened. His black, wavy hair stuck up in the back, and his bangs fell into his eyes. His thin mouth turned down, as his dark eyebrows drew close together. His storm cloud brewed, but she refused to back down, even when he took a step toward her. He towered over her. "That's enough, Carina. I think you need to leave."

Words caught in her throat. Her momma had always taught her that if she didn't have anything nice to say, don't say it all. She had bitten back hateful words during every fight, but she had done that long enough.

Pushing up the sleeves of the robe, Carina thrust up her chin and stood her ground. Normally, she would have cowered back from him and cast down her eyes. This time, she steeled herself for a fight. "Kiss my ass, Bart! I'm leaving but not because you told me to."

She pulled off the four-carat diamond engagement ring, placed her chewed gum on top of the ring, and threw it at him. "And you can shove this up yours."

She turned on her high heels and stormed out with every ounce of grace she could muster up. The tears threatened to spill, and she managed to hold them until slamming the door behind her. Once her feet hit the hall, the eye-rain ensued.

Chapter 7

Hotel Monteleone - 3rd floor hallway

New Orleans, LA

Saturday, December 24th, 2016

5:00 PM

Rad eased open the hotel room door as if expecting a reindeer to jump in front him. He looked up and down the hall, hoping to see Santa's sexy Christmas elf again. The empty corridor stared back at him in both directions, and an image of her wrapped around another man jabbed at his heart. Rolling his eyes, he shrugged off the jealousy.

She's not mine. Get over it, loser.

Still wearing his bright red Christmas boxers, he stepped out of his room, shut the door as quietly as possible and walked down the hall. The room had supplied a robe, but he had given it to the lady. While he kept his ear tuned and eyes peeled for other hotel guests, he had no idea where he would hide if someone ran into him. The ice machine room was only five doors down. What could go wrong?

Famous last words…

He sprinted down the hall to the ice machine, set the bucket in, and pressed the black button. Of course, nothing happened. He lightly hit the side of the silver machine and pressed again. Yet again, no whirr…no ice.

The elevator dinged, and he raised his head as he listened. A slurred voice belted out "Here Comes Santa Clause," and he hid behind a fake plant. Fortunately, the drunk stumbled past without looking his way.

Letting out the breath he'd been holding, Rad slammed his fist against the machine before pushing the button. The ice beast woke from its slumber, and the machine whirred into action. Cubes dropped into the bucket, filled it to the rim, and kept coming. He danced back a few steps to avoid the flying, frozen water chips. Before long, there was enough ice at his feet to build a snowman. The machine groaned, spit out a few more, and finally stopped.

Shaking his head, Rad stepped on ice to retrieve the bucket. Cold seeped into his bare feet, and shivers instantly shook his body. He jumped back and danced from one foot to another in an effort to warm up. He collided with a solid body, and he instantly turned to the left in an attempt to catch himself with the wall. He didn't want to crush anyone.

"Oh, man, I'm really sorry." Rad whipped around while he spewed the apology.

He stared into steel blue eyes with a few crinkles in the corners. The woman's soft, grey hair reached her shoulders, and her cupid mouth had laugh lines. The rest of her smooth face belied her age, as did her slim body. The elderly woman drew her robe together and raised her left eyebrow as she took in his lack of clothing. He wanted to crawl under a rock, but no self-respecting guy would flinch in this situation. So, he decided to own it instead.

Holding the ice bucket in front of his boxers, he puffed out his chest and lifted a corner of his mouth in his best sexy smirk. "Did Santa bring me a cougar for Christmas?"

The woman busted out laughing, and he released the breath he'd been holding. He had expected a firm reprimand, but she threw open her robe to reveal she wore a red two-piece bikini. For an older woman, he had to admit she still had a rocking body.

"Care to join us for a skinny dip, laddy?" Her Irish lilt tickled his ear, and he was beginning to wonder if he had bit off more than he could chew.

As he stammered for a reply, another attractive older woman stepped into view. "Iris, come on. Stop teasing the poor lad. We have to continue emptying our bucket list."

Iris closed her robe back, patted Rad on the wrist, and winked at him. "Next time, laddy. Merry Christmas."

The two disappeared down the hall, and Rad shook his head. *How do I always get myself into these messes?* From this to the unexpected Christmas gift ...

At the mere thought, a picture of the lady in her matching Christmas underwear popped into his head. Certain parts of him approved of the memory. If she were his girl, there was no way she would be alone on Christmas Eve. She would be dreaming of *his* sugar plums instead of dealing with the busy gingerbread man.

After he filled the ice bucket, Rad started back toward his room, fighting the urge to run because he feared another encounter with strangers. He rolled his eyes at himself. *It's New Orleans. No one cares you're in your boxers. In fact, I'm surprised I haven't run into anyone else dressed like this.*

The elevator dinged, and rowdy male voices echoed down the hall. Rad's heart lurched as he recognized their voices, and he increased his pace. He desired to see the lady again, not his drunken buds … especially now that he was half nude.

"Yo, it's Rad," hollered Chip.

"Ohhh Raddd, you look sexyyy." This came from his childhood friend, Darren.

He rolled his eyes and hesitated. A white clad figure moved toward him, but it was more important for him to turn and face the three men than see who the person was. His three buddies wavered toward him. The leader, Chip, was a blonde-haired, blue-eyed Casanova and always had women lusting after him as if he were a movie star. The other two trailed behind him. Sean, a spunky, redhaired Irishman, practically carried Darren, their black-haired friend.

"I'm so glad you boys finally recognize my sexual prowess." Shifting the ice bucket to his left hand, Rad gave them a thumbs up with his right. "Good night, fellas."

"Aw, come on. The night's young," Chip whined. "Jus' one more drink with us."

Rad shook his head and began back-pedaling toward his room. "G'night, y'all."

He swung around, right as the white clad figure ran in to him. He dropped the ice bucket to wrap his arms around the person, and ice scattered everywhere, including his feet. The person turned out to be his new-found woman friend. Her soft curves melted against him, as her body heat effectively destroyed the ice cubes crushed between them. She threw her arms around his neck. Tears streaked down her face, and a tiny sob escaped her mouth.

"I can't believe that lowlife nutria rat," she sobbed. Her hot lips pressed against his neck, and more shivers jolted down his body, but these weren't cold.

"Shhh, it's ok." He kicked the ice bucket out of the way and tried to get her walking toward his room. His current goal was to get away from the drunken trio behind him. She had other ideas.

"Two can play games ..." she whispered.

Her luscious warm lips pressed against his mouth, stopping his gentle maneuvers to walk her backwards toward his room. Her cinnamon flavored tongue encompassed every one of his thoughts. Her hand slipped up his neck, and her fingers played with his hair. The sweet sensations of touch and taste held him as if he were a reindeer stuck in Louisiana swamp mud. The only difference between him and the deer was that he didn't fight his bonds, choosing instead to sink deeper into her charm. His arms tightened around her, as he forgot about everything but the woman in his arms. Santa had indeed been kind to him this year.

"Look at Rad," called Chip. "Getting the rod on. Geaux, Rad."

Ignoring the catcalls from his friends, he cradled her back with his right arm, slipped his left under her legs, and swooped her up into his arms. She nuzzled her face against his bare chest, and her tongue tentatively darted against his nipple. Desire shot through him, and he nearly dropped her in shock. She clearly was out of her mind, and he had no desire to let her make a mistake she'd instantly regret.

Shifting her into a position that made her move her face to his neck, he took a tentative step forward, hoping that he could hide his own interest from her in the same motion. Several steps later, he reached his room, where he set her down, unlocked the door, and quickly ushered her in. He shut the door on Chip's leering face.

As he faced her, she threw herself at him. Her arms ensnared his neck, and she pressed her lips against his mouth, which instantly opened for her. Heat encompassed his senses, reminding him of a log going up in flames. He remained helpless for an instant as his candy cane caught fire and burned at his good intentions. His good senses finally dowsed the desire, and his hands firmly grasped her upper arms. As gently as possible, he moved her away, shaking his head.

"Much as my body says yes," he whispered. "We both know this would be a big mistake."

Chapter 8

Hotel Monteleone - Rad's hotel room # 333

New Orleans, LA

Saturday, December 24, 2016

5:15 PM

Carina clung to Rad as he carried her toward his room, burying her face in the curve of his neck. She inhaled his cologne, a fresh outdoorsy scent that appealed to her libido. Sensations sizzled into every nerve, diving straight down to her nether region. Her heart panged as she half hoped her former fiancé would step into the hall and see them. But then again, maybe that was a terrible idea. Of course, their parting words to each other hadn't been pleasant.

He had called her a controlling, workaholic nag, and she had called him a cheating freak and spit in his face. Well, spit toward his face, anyway. The saliva had landed on his bare chest and dripped over her chin. She had swiped her mouth dry and stormed out of the room in a rage.

She was glad they hadn't moved in together like he had wanted to six months ago. At least she wouldn't have to go through the agony of seeing him again, unless she had left anything in his apartment. She racked her brain, but all she could come up with was a toothbrush.

He could sit on that and spin for all I care.

Rad set her down, opened the door and ushered her in. She wished she didn't know that her ex was still in the room next door.

Fresh tears slid down her cheeks as she sat on the bed, sinking into the mattress.

Her newfound friend handed her a cup of water. "It's not a hot beverage like Sheldon suggests…"

She accepted the offer, and the humor but didn't feel like smiling. "I like that show too, but Bart hated it."

"Well, that's just sad for him," Rad sat beside her but made no move to touch her.

"I hope there's a lot of sadness for him," she murmured with her lips against the rim of the cup. She sipped the water but had trouble swallowing. Her stomach churned, and the icy water splashed into the acidic pit like an icicle dropped in a hot tub.

Lowering the cup, she noticed the way in which her hand was shaking, so she firmly grasped the cup to regain control. Her teeth chattered as an unnatural cold settled into her bones. Despite the bathrobe, goose bumps rose across her flesh, and her body shook.

Rad slipped an arm around her shoulders, and she stiffened. Part of her wanted to sink into his attention, but the other side of her was cautious. She didn't need to jump from one relationship into another.

"It's okay. I am not looking for more kisses…yet," he assured her. "Just think of me as a brother."

She looked at him out of the corner of her eye, admiring the curve of his jaw. "Um, yeah, no."

He laughed. "Best friend then?"

"Best friends are a myth…especially when they're the opposite sex." Even *she* heard the loneliness in her words. Did she

45

really think that, and when had she started believing that? She thought about how many females she had ever considered as something close to a best friend. They added up on one hand. Of course, she and Bart had been close at one time, but lately that gap had widened. Now she knew why. She should have trusted her gut, which told her lovers can't be best friends.

"Let's just leave it as friends then," Rad said softly. "And as one friend to another, you look like you need something stronger than a cup of water."

Carina stared forlornly at the cup's contents. She grunted. "I think you're right."

Rad stood, and the mattress shifted. Kneeling in front of the tiny fridge, he held up a bottle of wine. "The cheapest money can buy."

The fridge door clunked shut as he rose. Twisting off the cap, he poured wine into two plastic cups and held it out. Carina took it, and before he could propose a toast, she downed it. Sour fruitiness tingled over her tongue, and she pursed her mouth and shuddered.

"Sorry," Rad said. "My friends drank the good stuff before the night began."

"It's ok. I…" She looked around the room, suddenly realizing she was alone with a complete stranger. "I guess I need to call downstairs and see if they have a room. There's no way I can drive back to Baton Rouge right now."

He shook his head. "I know we just met, and you don't know me. But I promise I won't try anything. There are two beds…"

Weariness clung to her like a warm blanket on a cold winter day. The adrenaline rush was fading, and she held out the empty cup. "More wine, please."

He obliged and also took the water cup from her. "How long were y'all together?"

"Seven years and some odd months. Guess this is the itch everyone talks about." Carina downed the wine. "This was a dumb idea. If I hadn't come down here—"

"We never would have met," Rad interrupted. "And I am glad we did."

He refilled their cups, emptying the bottle. He raised his glass. "To new and unexpected friendships."

She tapped her cup against his and once again downed the wine. Warm fuzzies crept over her, and she closed her eyes. Her heart constricted as if it shriveled into a raisin, and her lungs froze, capturing her breath. At one time, she and Bart had been best friends. Perhaps that's what had tarnished her perspective on friendship. The women she knew just didn't get her. Only a handful had, and Bart had done a fine job of pretending to understand her. In retrospect, she realized he had been faking for the last several years. Their communication had resorted to basic words of 'Hey, how are you? What's for dinner?' and 'I'm going on a business trip.' Long talks into the night had vanished.

"You're my honeybunch," sang the pillow to her right. "Sugar plum, pumpy-umpy-umpkin, you're my sweetie pie. You're my cuppycake, gumdrop Snoogums, boogums, you're the apple of my eye."

Rad's eyes widened, and his face turned red. He frantically pushed the pillow off the bed to reveal his cell phone. A picture of a beautiful, elderly woman flashed on the screen along with the words *Mommy's calling*. He snatched it up, sliding his finger across the ignore button.

A corner of Carina's mouth lifted into a smile as their eyes met. He lifted his shoulders and rolled his eyes. The phone began singing the Cuppycake song again. He backed pedaled to the bathroom.

"If I don't answer this, she'll never stop calling." He shut the door, but Carina could still hear him. "Mom, what is it? Yes, I'm in my hotel room…yes, I'm behaving. Mom, I'm a twenty-seven-year-old man. I know how to keep my nose clean. I promise I'm being a good boy…I love you, too. Good night…Yes, I'm still your little oompa loompa."

Something about the way he said that caused Carina to pause. She tilted her head and narrowed her eyes as a vague memory tapped at her brain. The way Rad had ended the conversation reminded her of a boy she'd known years ago. Of course, in her mind, that boy still had braces, big black plastic glasses, and wore a size 3X t-shirt.

Carina let out a tiny breath that erupted into a deep sigh. *Another friendship ruined. When will one last? I'm never going to keep one best friend outside of a family setting. I need to just stop trying. It's just pointless. Besides, no way is there any possibility of this guy and that boy being the same person.*

She stewed for a second, then went to retrieve her cell phone from her suitcase. *Perhaps old Hot Dog is on social media.*

Half expecting to pop out of the bathroom, she tapped her foot as her phone took forever to boot up. When the phone sprang to life, she listened for signs of Rad exiting but only heard running water.

Why am I worrying if he's going to catch me? It's none of his business why I'm on my phone.

Pushing down the sense of being sneaky, she looked for her old high school friend online, but nothing popped up. However, she knew she had a few pics on her own page. After scrolling through a few thousand photos, she finally found the one she wanted. She squinted at it, trying to see some resemblance to the man in the bathroom.

"What's got you so preoccupied?" Rad's voice carried from the bathroom, where he stood in the entranceway. The light caressed his skin, and all Carina could think of was running her hands over his biceps and down his chest. Her fingertips wiggled, imaging the exploration of other squishier parts of him.

Oh, this is not how friends react to one another. Soooo not a good sign

Chapter 9

Hotel Monteleone - Rad's hotel room # 333

New Orleans, LA

Saturday, December 24, 2016

5:15 PM

Rad pushed the call end button on his phone, and shaking his head, he set the phone on the counter instead of in the ice bucket. He loved his mom, and he didn't blame her for being a worry wart. He had put her through Hell during his rebellious years, but they had all made it to the other side virtually unscathed. Many of his other friends still lived dangerously, and for the most part, he had moved on to different friends.

Of course, the group he had come down here with was part of the dangerous crowd, but he wasn't about to let them ruin what had taken him several years to build up. He owned his own business. Antique furniture had become very profitable, especially after the great flood of East Baton Rouge and the surrounding parishes. Many people didn't trust that the item had not been flooded, but it's extremely difficult to hide evidence of flood, especially on wood. Unfortunately, it required hands on purchases instead of buying via the internet, which meant more travelling for him and more responsibility for his employees.

He picked up his phone, took a selfie of himself in the bathroom mirror with a date and time stamp then sent it to his mom. He typed: *I'm being good. Love you!*

After using the facilities and splashing some water on his face, Rad opened the door to see Carina had made herself at home on the spare bed. What a delicious sight she made. Maybe he should take a picture of *that* and send it to his mom. He closed his eyes and shook his head. *Down, bad boy, you died years ago. Mom doesn't deserve anymore torture.*

"What's got you so preoccupied?" he asked, standing in the bathroom doorway.

Carina stared at him as if he were meat on a platter. Her mouth fell open as her desire played over her face. Dropping her gaze, she pointed to the suitcase by the hotel window. "I'm so glad you didn't throw that out. I didn't realize I had left it."

He nodded. "I figured you'd be back for it sooner or later...especially after I heard you chewing his ass out. Good for you. He deserved it."

She looked down at the phone in her lap and twisted her mouth. Something about the way she hesitated made him curious, but he waited patiently as she figured out what she was stewing on. The moment stretched into uncomfortable silence, but he enjoyed watching her squirm. The sight of her teeth nibbling on her lower lip sent his thoughts to something else being nibbled on. He considered going back into the bathroom for a cold shower. Or even a trip down the hall to play in the melting ice.

She held her phone up. "Is this you?"

His eyes widened, and his cheeks turned red. It was his horrible high school picture, and not one on Facebook. He was surprised that she kept it on her phone. Such a personal gesture for someone he hadn't seen since a year after graduation. He had hoped she wouldn't have recognized him just yet. He had known whom she was the minute she popped out of the box, and at first, he had thought she had remembered him, too. Of course, that had instantly been squelched.

"Hey, C-witch." Rad used her high school nickname because she had been fascinated with witches at the time. He paused before singing. "It's been a long time. You're just as lovely as you used to be."

Her head inclined to the right as her arms folded over one another. "Singing George Jones to me won't explain why you disappeared without saying a word to me."

Rad lifted both hands with palms up and his shoulders lifted toward his ears. "You were deep in a relationship and didn't need me. I found other things to do."

Her eyes looked up at the ceiling as a huff escaped her lips. "That dude turned out to be a bigger warlock than I bargained for. I don't do satanic rituals, and he opened my eyes to things I did not want to participate in. I could have used a true friend to vent to. You even changed your cell phone number."

He raised his hands up in surrender. "I was in the middle of a complete life change myself. I went out of state to live with my uncle on his farm, lost the weight, learned a trade, and came back to Baton Rouge a different man. I got back to my country roots and away from all that goth crap."

Carina set her phone down, lay back, and pulled the covers up to her chin. She stared at the ceiling. "I blame that on Bart, but I really don't want to talk about that jerk right now."

Rad checked the locks on the door. "So, now that we're not complete strangers like you thought, do you feel safe enough to stay here with me?"

"It's a little early to go to sleep." Her words trailed off to a whisper as she buried her head in the pillow. "I can't stay in this room knowing he is right there." She threw her hand toward the wall behind her bed.

Rad heard the pain in her voice, and his heart went out to her. He refrained from rushing to her side. *If my friends knew what a softy I am…*

"You're not planning on driving back to BR tonight, are you? You've had a few drinks and aren't in any condition to drive … given your emotional state." He slipped into the other bed, turned on his side, and propped his head on his left hand. He stuck out his tongue and crossed his eyes. "You can't say no to this face."

Two short giggles filled her throat. "Same old Hot Dog"

Rad pushed out his lower lip. "Not funny."

"Ah, come on, Conrad. You know I'm just teasing you." She turned on her side but rested her head on the pillow. Her brunette hair spread over it, reminding him of corn silk from his uncle's farm. He used to love to braid her hair when they were teenagers.

"I have to fess up," she whispered. Her chin tucked closer to her chest as her eyes looked at her lap.

"You thought I was into guys." His smile faded to a deep frown. He wondered if the old hurt showed in his eyes.

"I…I never said that." Carina fidgeted with the bedcover, obviously squirming from the truth.

53

"But I knew you thought it. A lot of people did. Truth was…I couldn't have the girl I wanted, so I tried to push you away…successfully, it seems."

She lowered her eyelids as a frown appeared on her face. Then her cheeks turned bright red, and she abruptly sat up. Her green eyes swirled with sudden clarity. "Oh…Oh dear. I had no idea."

Rad waved his hand. "It's okay. I'm over you. Had my own little series of misadventures in love."

Her head tilted again, and her hair fell away from her neck, exposing a luscious curve he wanted to explore. She squinched her face as if struggling to remember something. "Weren't you dating some crud, goth chic at the time?"

My turn to squirm.

Rad scrunched his nose and scratched his right ear. His face heated, and he hid it briefly in the pillow before peeking out at her. "Gawd, can't believe you remembered that."

"I remember a lot of things…good and bad." Her mouth pursed briefly before a yawn overtook her. She sank back down onto her pillow. "I'm sorry."

"For what?" His head sank into the soft pillow, reminding him of softer things of hers. He squelched the thought as best he could, but the briefest memory of her *things* started revving up his fire.

Ice cream…snow…ice…wicked witch…but in the new version, she's pretty hot too. He stifled a groan.

"The way we parted. You were right, and I was wrong. Neither of us approved of each other's love interests. I wish I could have told you sooner. Seems like all I do is make Christmas mistakes."

Rad sat up and rubbed the back of his neck, unable to take his eyes off Carina. The blanket was tucked around her body, showing all her lovely bumps and curves. He shook his head to free his brain of the intruding, wanton thoughts. His eyebrows squished together. "What do you mean by that?"

"Well, today of course." She refused to look at him. "And then the last time I saw or talked to you was on Christmas Day…when I slammed the door in your face for breaking my phone."

Chapter 10

Carina's Home

Baton Rouge, LA

December 24, 2005, Saturday

4:00 pm

"Carina, girl, you are seriously jumping the couch!" Conrad's voice screamed out of the cell phone. She cringed at the anger that pulsed in his words. "Don't you dare tell me who to date."

"Don't you compare me to that old fart Tom Cruise." Seventeen-year-old Carina held the hot pink flip phone away from her ear. She pressed her lips over the intercom holes. "Hot Dog, you need to chill. I care about you, but that…rotten candy cane of a girlfriend you have? That's a Halloween story, not a Christmas one."

He grunted so loud, she thought he'd scratch his throat in the process. "Ugh! Just because you saw a picture of her on Myspace kissing another dude does not mean it happened recently."

Carina paced in front of the family television. Fortunately, her mother was next door at her aunt's, so the house was empty. She had no brothers or sisters to bother her. Sometimes that was a blessing, but she did get lonely. Right now, Hot Dog was the closest thing to a sibling that she had, and she felt him slipping right through her fingers.

"Get out of your car and come inside. I will prove it." She snapped the cover down on her phone, effectively hanging up on her best friend.

If they couldn't be honest with each other, who could they be honest with? They had been best friends since ninth grade. He had her back. She had his.

Holding open the door, she stepped aside to let in Big Hot Dog. He was four inches taller than her, which put him at five foot nine. However, his nickname was derived from his weight of three hundred pounds. He wore black from his hoodie to his jeans to his lipstick. His spiked blonde hair was tipped with black.

Carina sighed inwardly at the sight of her country boy turned goth. His current girlfriend had gotten her raven claws deeper into him than anyone. She suspected he had delved into more than just drinking beer and dipping tobacco. She feared the goth girl had gotten him to smoke pot… and even more so, introducing him to a dark side that she wouldn't be able to help him come back from.

"Well, where's the proof?" Hot Dog crossed his arms. His foot tapped, ironically to the music video blasting from the television: Gwen Stefani's Hollaback Girl." The song was appropriate since they were hollering at one another.

Carina tossed her long hair over her shoulder and closed the door. Flipping open her phone, she pulled up a picture. "I took this last night at the T-Club. Brad and I were there with some of his friends."

Hot Dog's blue eyes rolled up and over as if he were following a rainbow from one end to another. "Who are now your friends…"

Her right fist clenched. His pettiness over her new set of friends irked her to no end. At least they weren't leading her down a dark path to trouble. Ignoring his tone of jealousy, she held the phone up to his face. "See? It was before the crowd got there."

Hot Dog raised his thick black glasses and squinted at the phone. He took it out of her hand. After a second of studying it, he made a grunting oof sound, his signature sound of disbelief. "Can't even see their faces. Your phone sucks."

Stepping back a few feet, he tossed it back at her. Lights from the tree sparkled across the pink case as it flew through the aromatic air. A nearby candle chose that moment to waft its cinnamon scent under her nose. She dove for the phone, but she missed the catch. Her prized possession clattered against the ceramic-tiled floor. The top broke with a snap, and Carina's anger flared.

"Freakin' great, Hot Dog! I can't believe you broke my phone. You're such a clutz!" She waved her hands at him.

"I'm not the one who missed the catch." The big man-child crossed his thick arms and stared down his nose at her.

"You did it on purpose." Her hands balled up into fists as she screamed at him. She stomped both her feet as if trying to squash a spider.

His face clouded over with even more darkness. His mouth set in a thin line, and his eyebrows drew together, causing his forehead to wrinkle. "No, I didn't."

His big foot stomped on the phone, rendering it a mess of metal. "But *that* totally was on purpose."

"No!" Tears sprang to her eyes as her rage flew off the deep end. "Get out of my house. I never want to see you again."

Hot Dog hesitated, regret flashing over his face. His mouth opened and closed before anger replaced regret. "Fine with me."

He stormed to the door, opened it, and stepped outside. Turning back, he snarled, "And your choice in boyfriends sucks, too. You've turned into a stuck-up carrot that sits on top Frosty's face."

She only partially heard his hurtful words. Her heart crumbled as her fingers hovered over the crushed phone. The hole in her heart opened wide, and grief wrapped its arms around her, suffocating not only her lungs but her soul as well. Wounds from the loss of a loved one take time to heal, and this one was still fresh.

"The last picture of me and my dad is on that phone," Carina cried as she picked up the pieces of phone.

Tears welled up and spilled out of the corners of her eyes, trailing down her cheeks like melting snow. Her dad had died earlier that year...a day after Hurricane Katrina hit. He had been a captain of a shrimp boat, and the stubborn man had gone to New Orleans to check on his boat where it was being worked on. One of the twin motors had died, and he wanted to be sure the boat was still there. Nobody wanted him to go, but it was his only means of income. He had to find out if the boat was safe.

Looters were in the process of stealing from the deserted boat shop. From the police reports, he had tried to hold them with his own registered firearm, but the punks got it away from him. They shot him in the forehead and stole his Ford F-150 truck. He had died instantly, and Carina still could not wrap her head around the fact that he was gone. Sometimes, she pretended he was simply gone shrimping.

"I'm sorry," Hot Dog said quietly.

Her heart panged as she looked up at him. The glasses and goth makeup hid his facial features, so all she saw was his scowl. His hands twisted around each other, but she refused to acknowledge the tell-tale sign of his worry. It flitted over her brain, but she was tired of everything— her friend, her life, her family…her dad's death.

Sometimes grief took a long time to heal, and for her, she knew deep down that this death would be one she never got over. She literally bounced into anger. Jumping to her feet, she rushed over and pushed him further away from the house.

"I don't ever want to see you again," she screamed as she slammed the door in his face or tried to. His big foot blocked the door from completely closing. If it hurt, his face didn't show it.

"I said I am sorry," Hot Dog yelled. "I told you months ago to save that picture somewhere else. You never listen to me. Especially now with that … that prep-head all up in your ears. I will take Sassy any day over your…your…stupid new boyfriend."

Carina swiped at the steady stream coming out of her eyes. All she wanted was to go hide in her bed and throw the covers over her head. She leaned against the door, trying to push it closed despite the foot still lodged in the way. Exhausted and heartbroken, she resorted to resting her body against as she waited for him to stop yelling at her.

"Hot Dog…please…stop." She heard the weariness in her words…almost as if she were listening to someone else. A loud sob caught in her throat, and it was almost her undoing.

"He's gone, ReRe. He ain't coming back. Get over it already," Hot Dog continued relentlessly.

"Go away," she whispered. "Please...stop."

Silence covered both of them. Music blasted from the television, and the grandfather clock next to the door ticked louder than she remembered it being. Her heart thudded rapidly against her ribs like the wings of a hummingbird.

The door shifted as he pulled his foot out. She straightened up and slammed it shut. The noise echoed above the music, and she cringed, certain her mother had heard all the way next door. She focused on the shadowy figure on the other side of the curtained window. He wasn't moving, and she lost it.

"Get lost," she screamed at the top of her lungs.

The figure disappeared, and she crumpled to the ground, succumbing to grief.

Chapter 11

Carina's Driveway

Baton Rouge, LA

December 24, 2005, Saturday

4:20 pm

Rad

Hot Dog stared at Carina's door. Her silhouette leaned against the window as her shoulders shook. Her pitiful sobs tore at his heart, and he struggled with wanting to comfort her and needing to get the Christmas bells out of there.

He couldn't believe he had just lost his best friend. He didn't know why he had let his anger get the better of him. Things were spiraling out of control for him, and he felt as if he were stuck inside a tornado.

Why did I do that? Stupid, stupid, stupid…

The weight of his actions pressed down on him as if the Grinch had dumped all the stolen gifts on top of him. He slunk back to his car, got in, and rummaged through the trash on the passenger seat. Finding the cigarette pack, he lit one up and inhaled deeply. Closing his eyes, he savored the menthol filling up his lungs. Too bad it didn't calm him as much as it used to. Other things had taken the place, and thoughts of getting a puff of weed filled his head.

Shutting the door, he cranked the car and hesitated. He looked toward Carina's house, hoping to see her running to stop him. Only brown, dead leaves raced across the driveway, pushed by the wind.

"Damn," he whispered. An image of his black shoe stomping the pink cell phone flashed in his head.

Her dad had been an awesome dude. They had gone fishing and had gotten along. In fact, the picture she referred to had been of all three of them. They had held their big, red fish up proudly for the camera. The size of those reds would have given a pelican a run for its money had the bird tried to eat one of them.

Taking a drag, he blew out a puff a smoke. And as for his girlfriend, Carina was wrong. That picture was not of Jayda. No way. His little dark jewel would not be caught dead in a country bar. Besides, just last night, she had said those three little words to him. Of course, they had been pretty stoned so…had she really meant it? Or was she just happy that he had scored them some good stuff?

Hot Dog glanced one more time at the empty kitchen window before throwing the car into reverse. He peeled out of the drive, putting as much distance between himself and his old life as fast as possible. Time to figure out the world with Jayda by his side. They were leaving for California that night, and nothing and nobody would stand in his way.

He pushed all thoughts of and feelings for Carina into a tiny box, locked it, and threw the key into the darkest recesses of his mind. He was a grown man. Eighteen and graduated. Time to do something with that guitar of his, and with Jayda by his side, his voice would land a record deal in no time.

Hot Dog stomped on the gas pedal and made the tires squeal down the pavement. He could care less if the entire neighborhood heard. He hoped the sound of it pissed off ReRe, too.

Ten minutes later, he pulled onto a dirt driveway located on Hubbs Road, north of Central. Bare trees crowded the small shack of a house, and brown leaves covered the ground. The place needed a few coats of paint, and the carport needed someone to throw a garage sale. There was so much stuff that the cars couldn't park in it, which led to grease spots on the dead, brown grass in various places. A handful of junk cars were also strewn about. If it weren't for weeds popping out of broken windows, it would be difficult to tell a working car from a dead one.

Jayda lived here with several family members— more than what would comfortably fit inside the shack. Most of the time, she slept on the porch swing. Very rarely was she ever alone when home.

A string of Christmas lights outlined the porch. Many of the bulbs were burned out ... probably because they stayed on year-round. Jayda's family was as lazy as dirt on a dog.

Hot Dog turned off the engine, threw open the door and struggled to get out. Sadness darted over him as he considered it amazing that he fit inside the car at all. Once he managed to get out, he rested his hand on car roof, struggling to catch his breath.

Would Nashville even take me seriously? I gotta get this weight off.

He had struggled with it all of his life and was envious of those who didn't know what it was like to battle the insane love affair with eating. He practically lived at fast food restaurants, even making midnight runs to cave into his desires. *What would this world be like if we had never invented drive through food?*

A deep sigh escaped his lips as he eyed the unopened bag of potato chips on the passenger seat. Closing his eyes, he pushed away from the car, wondering if Jayda would help him, hoping beyond hope that she would.

Carina would if I had asked...well, before this afternoon, anyway...

When he reached the front porch, he grabbed the rail and hauled himself up the four steps. Loud voices, the sound from a television show and music blared from the house. The inhabitants wouldn't hear his heavy steps on the creaky boards, much less his knock. He didn't bother and let himself in.

To his right was the living room, and bodies lay sprawled from tattered couches to the dirty floor. None were his girl, so he continued down the hall toward the kitchen. Just before he got there, the bathroom door opened, and out she stepped. She stopped dead in her tracks, and her deep green eyes stared at him in surprise. She pulled the door tight behind her as she stumbled for words. He thought someone else was in there, but he couldn't see who. He assumed it was her sister.

"Hot Dog," Jayda gushed. "You're early."

She refused to look him in the eye, and he noticed how bright pink her cheeks were. However, her hair wasn't wet, and she was dressed. So that ruled out a shower.

Maybe she's simply overheated. There never is enough air condition coming from those weak-ass window units.

He shrugged and ran a hand through his hair. "Yeah, just ready to blow this town."

She held up a finger. "Can you give me half an hour?"

He nodded, drinking in the sight of her delicate, black tinged lips. "You got it, babe. Is there a spot in the kitchen? The living room is filled to capacity."

Wrapping her arms in a self-hug, Jayda's hands rubbed her forearms as if she were cold. She shifted from one foot to the other, and her teeth bit her bottom lip. "Actually, no. Can you wait in the car for me? I promise I won't be long."

Hot Dog thought about the bag of chips. "Sure thing, babe."

She stood on her tippy toes and planted a kiss on his cheek. "Thanks. Be there shortly."

He made a hasty exit, glad to escape the tiny house and all its cringe-worthy people. He didn't particularly like any of her family. They all seemed like leeches to him. Climbing into the car, he opened the chips and watched the porch, waiting for his girl to emerge.

Five minutes later, a dude that he had never seen before came out. The guy looked straight at him, and Hot Dog's eyes narrowed as a feeling of familiarity flitted over him. *Where have I seen that guy before?*

Ducking his head, the guy danced down the steps to a truck parked by the end of the driveway. Two minutes later, Jayda came out and watched him leave. Hot Dog looked from her to the guy, wondering if the guy was her friend, but as she got in the car, she batted her lashes at Hot Dog. All thoughts except being with her fled from his brain.

She threw her bag in the back seat and faced him. Bouncing on the seat, she settled on her knees as her soft hands cradled his face. Still refusing to look him in the eye, she closed hers and planted a deep, sweet kiss on him. All he could think of was how delicious she tasted.

All too soon, she withdrew the gift of her lips and pulled away from him. She wiped her mouth with her left fingers as she settled back in the passenger seat and buckled up. "You ready to set Nashville on fire, darling?"

He smiled as he fought back the nagging tinge in the back of his brain that said something wasn't right. He should have listened to it, but everything happens for a reason. "Let's do this."

Chapter 12

Hotel Monteleone - Rad's hotel room # 333

New Orleans, LA

Saturday, December 24, 2016

5:30 PM

Carina

"Well, Jayda was apparently good for you. Look how well you turned out." Carina remained tucked under the blanket and lifted her hand off her hip to wave in his direction.

Rad choked on a laugh. "This was not her doing...well maybe in a way. She and I split up a year later. By then, her friends— my *so-called* friends— led me on a bad path. Fortunately, I realized I had to get off that path before something bad happened. Unfortunately, that meant giving up the guitar hero gig."

Carina tilted her head. "So, this hotel *isn't* paid for by your famous career in music?"

He chuckled. "Gawd, I haven't thought about that fiasco in years." She pointed to the guitar in the corner. "But you still play..."

"Just for kicks. That life is toxic and not for me. I will stick to beer, slow women, and making memories at the home front." He threw back the covers and sat up. "I'm famished. Let's go get something to eat. Is there anywhere in particular you'd like to go?"

At the mention of food, her stomach protested its emptiness. Some fried shrimp would hit the spot. "How about The Court of Two Sisters?"

He rubbed his belly. "Sounds good."

68

Carina got out of the other bed. "Let me put on something decent."

She got her tiny suitcase, rolled it into the bathroom, and shut the door. It didn't take her long to change and freshen up. As she reapplied makeup over her tearstained cheeks, her heart lodged in her throat. She pushed aside the feeling and the image of Brad being just on the other side of the wall. She had to get out of here but did not want to go home. That would be a long and horrible drive. Being alone tonight was the last thing she wanted.

She opened the door. "I'm ready."

"Me, too," Rad said as he slipped on his brown corduroy jacket.

"Wow," she whistled. "Long cry from the black hoodie wearing youth…"

"Psht, I was always country. I just got lost for a while. Made my way back to my roots, and boy am I glad I did." He juggled his cell phone in the air. "Can I get your number? Just in case we get separated…"

After they exchanged info, he tucked his cell phone in his pocket. "Are you ready?"

Carina nodded as she slipped on her purple cardigan. "Ready as 'Hard Candy Christmas,'" she sang.

He held open the door. "Come on, Dolly Parton."

When they got to the elevator, Rad pushed the button and faced her. "I *am* sorry I stepped on your phone."

Carina shrugged. "It was just a phone. I shouldn't have gotten so upset."

"No, I get it. You thought you lost the last pic of you and your dad."

The elevator dinged, and the doors opened to reveal an old couple holding hands and singing "Baby, It's Cold Outside." The sight was sweet, and somehow, Carina felt prophetic of a future yet to be. She looked at Rad, and the sorrow in his eyes made her wince. She placed a palm on his stubbled cheek, and the touch sent a cozy fire through her skin.

"Seriously, it is not a big deal. I got over it." Her hand slipped away from his face, and she stepped into the elevator.

Rad followed, and as the doors closed, he pulled out his phone. Seconds later, her phone dinged, and she looked at him with a smile, wondering what joke he had sent about the still singing old couple.

When she tapped on his text, her mouth dropped. It was the lost picture of her dad.

"What…how…" she stammered.

"I had a copy, too. I mean, I am in the picture."

Carina stared at her dad, who was forty in the picture. It was the weekend before Hurricane Katrina hit, and the three of them had gone fishing. At the time, Rad's hair was his natural color of brown, and he wore a flannel shirt. He hadn't hit the goth fiasco until after her dad died.

The elevator doors swung open, and they exited through a small crowd, waiting to get on. The next few minutes were spent weaving through the streets of the French Quarter. The smell of beer and fried food permeated the air. The nightly city party was well under way.

Carina's heart warmed as she contemplated Rad's text. She was surprised he had saved it but even more surprised at his transformation. Some people stay the same after high school, but some changed.

Rad stopped next to a line of people that began under a black and white sign for The Court of Two Sisters restaurant. He closed his eyes and inhaled the aroma of food. "I hope the wait isn't too long. I am famished. It's a shame we missed the buffet."

Carina nodded. "Me, too. Normally I am not a fan of buffets, but this one is top notch."

During the wait and through the meal, Carina and Rad reminisced about the good old days before the big falling out. Time melted like butter in a saucepan, and before long, they were strolling the streets. When they got to the corner of St. Charles Street and Carondelet, Rad grabbed her hand and pulled her in-between traffic to get to the median. Cars honked, people hollered, and drunks danced in their path. They skirted around all obstacles toward a green, red, and gold decorated streetcar that was taking on passengers, and they climbed on board. Rad paid for the ride as he had paid for dinner, and they took two empty seats at the back.

Most of the other riders were tourists with a few native New Orleans on their way home from work. When the singing began, Rad and Carina joined in. The impromptu Christmas carols ranged from "Jingle Bells" to "Silent Night."

When they neared the Garden District, the streetcar driver turned off the interior lights so they could see the old home decorated for the holidays. It was a sight to behold. There were

71

grand displays of Papa Noel in his pirogue with eight alligators pulling the craft. One home had a version of Mr. Bingle, a snowman designed by a long extinct department store, Maison Blanche, on Canal Street. Another had Christmas embellished swamp creatures around a tiny shack. The alligators and nutria rats gave gifts to the baby Jesus, who was tucked into a tiny wooden pirogue.

They rode the St. Charles streetcar from one end of the city to the other— from Carondelet to S Carrolton and back. They chatted for hours and almost missed their drop off. They went back to the hotel, and Carina fell asleep in the other bed with only a smidgeon of a thought of Bart. Her old friend had done a great job of taking her mind of the unpleasantness of earlier.

As she stared at Rad's sleeping face, she actually fell asleep with a smile rather than tears, and her dreams brought her back to a time of carefree youth where she and Hot Dog sat on the front of the boat. They rode the waves, laughing when one would send them off the seat or spray saltwater in their faces and up their noses. Her dad loved being their chauffeur and captain as they made the Gulf of Mexico their playground.

Chapter 13

Hotel Monteleone - Rad's hotel room # 333

New Orleans, LA

Sunday, December 25, 2016

9:00 AM

Carina

Carina's eyes fluttered open as sunlight crashed into her nightmare. Her heart ached as the remnants echoed in her brain. She had stumbled into Bart's room, filled with rage. When she went to scream at him, her mouth was covered with duct tape. Frustration filled her as she couldn't give him a piece of her mind.

Thankfully, that hadn't happened. She threw an arm over her eyes, groaning.

"Merry Christmas, C-witch."

The smell of hot coffee permeated the room. Her mouth watered, and her stomach gurgled. Moving her arm, she peeked at Rad. He stood between the beds, holding a tray adorned with a fancy mug that held a peppermint stick. Steam rolled from the cup, swirling up.

"Sit up. I worked hard to get this fresh, hot brew for you." His mouth tilted into a smile.

Carina stretched, sat up and accepted her first Christmas gift. "Thanks. I'm sorry I didn't get you anything." She smiled.

"Aw, I was hoping for a classic mustang." Rad stuck out his lower lip before giving her a knowing smile and a wink. "But I'll settle for the memory of you in your Christmas undies."

Resisting the urge to throw a pillow at him, Carina stuck out her tongue. She sipped the hot coffee, relishing the smooth flavor as it slid down her throat. "Yum."

"So," Rad said as he sat on the edge of the other bed. He wore faded blue jeans and a black t-shirt with a picture of Darth Vader in Santa's sleigh, led by eight AT-AT walkers wearing reindeer antlers heading toward the Death Star. "What are your plans? I can find out when your ex and his…um…well, find out when they check out or leave. Or you can lounge around here all day and mope…or hang out with me if you'd like."

She studied his face and took another sip of coffee. She wanted to run next door and kick some more butt. Of course, she also wanted to throw the covers back over her head and cry like rain hitting the Mississippi River. What good would either do? She was stronger than that and a better person.

"Since you didn't get me anything for Christmas," Rad drawled with a sexy wink. "My vote is for time."

Carina nibbled her lower lip as she weighed her options. She took another sip of coffee and nodded. "Okay, Hot Dog LeBlanc, I am yours for the day." She snickered and shook her head.

Rad tilted his head. "What?"

"I should've recognized you by your last name. What is wrong with me?"

"If my opinion counts, not a damn thing. Now get dressed. We have a city to explore."

Thirty minutes later, the doorman let Rad and Carina out of The Hotel Monteleone. The cold air rushed over Carina's face, and she pulled her heavy purple cardigan close to her neck. She knew once they started walking, her body heat would adjust. Rad stepped close to her but refrained from slipping his hand in hers. Something told her that he wanted to and part of her wanted him to, but she needed this to be kept a friendship. No rebound with her former best friend. She'd rather they catch up and resume the closeness they once shared before she'd screwed up.

"So where are we headed?" she asked, upping her naturally slow pace to match his long-legged stride.

"Wherever Santa brings us." He slowed down. "And that means no rushing."

They meandered down the sidewalks, letting people who were in a hurry pass. The French Quarter was decorated to the hilt for Christmas— red bows wrapped around old fashioned wrought iron lampposts, wreaths and garlands hung on the balconies of homes and businesses, and santa even passed. He waved at them from his seat in the cart behind a bicycle that was driven by a sexy woman dressed in an elf costume.

An elderly couple stood in front of a closed shop. The man had his arm around his sweetheart's waist as they admired the window display. Christmas dolls stared out of the shop with their hands in frozen waves. A Christmas train ran around them, little puffs of steam spewing out of it every now and then. It even whistled.

Rad and Carina watched for a moment before moving on. He chuckled. "Good thing you hadn't been delivered to their hotel room."

Carina's face reddened. "Oh my."

"The sight of you in your holiday outfit would have given that old man a HARD attack," he chuckled.

She slapped his shoulder. "Stop it."

"HARDiac arrest." Rad laughed.

She giggled, picturing the shock on the old man's face. His wife wouldn't have been too pleased. Well, maybe...maybe not. Who knew these days?

They walked for a while, window shopped a lot, caught up on each other's lives, discussed other classmates, and talked about movies and music. They both still liked the same stuff, and Carina admitted she had gone back to listening to country music.

"I still flip flop," she stated. "It depends on the mood I'm in."

They stood under the sign for The Court of Two Sisters, and her stomach rumbled. "I wish they were open. Last night's meal was da bomb."

"Me, too. They have the best buffet ever," Rad said as he stared forlornly through the closed iron gates.

Carina pulled out her phone and Googled for a decent place to eat. "It's Christmas Day, but there has to be somewhere good to eat lunch. We both deserve a good hot meal. No hot dogs."

He rubbed his belly. "I'd settle for a shrimp PoBoy."

"There are several close by— Broussard's Restaurant & Courtyard...Kingfish...Pizza Domenica." She met his eyes. "I know you love pizza but not today."

He laughed. "Still my guilty pleasure!"

She continued naming restaurants. "BourBe...what's that?"

His eyes lit up. "You've never been there?"

"No."

He grabbed her hand and led her down Royal Street. "Hopefully we can get in. Show starts in thirty minutes."

She raised her left eyebrow at him. "What kind of place is this?"

"It's nice...tasteful. BourBe stands for BourBesque. Their Sunday brunch is called Eggs a la Legs."

"Legs?"

He nodded. "It's a Burlesque Brunch."

Carina stopped in her tracks. "I'm not eighteen anymore. I don't care to visit..."

He held up his hand. "If you don't feel comfortable, then we can leave, but their food is incredible and reasonable."

She put her hands on her hips. "I can splurge on an upscale restaurant. It *is* Christmas, after all."

Rad smirked and crossed his arms. "So, this is your treat then?"

She nodded, grabbed his hand, and led him. "And no offense to your choice, but after the show I saw last night in Bart's room, I'd rather go to Broussard's."

Chapter 14

Jackson Square, French Quarter

New Orleans, LA

Sunday, December 25, 2016

2:00 PM

Rad

Despite it being Christmas Day, Jackson Square had a good crowd. Rad strolled beside Carina, and he snuck glances at her sweet face. He couldn't believe his luck. Santa had delivered a long overdue Christmas wish, but from past experiences with other girls— er— women, he was going to take this one slow. He had ruined his chances and their friendship when they were eighteen, but this time, he would take his time, even if it meant just being her friend for a while. He did not want to be Rebound Rad ever again. Past experiences with other women had taught him that valuable lesson. If friendship was all they ever had, then he could live with that. He hoped, anyway. He did not desire having another door literally slammed in his face by his first love.

"I'm stuffed," Carina moaned. "Why did you let me eat all that food?"

"And let you waste a perfectly good plate of Southern Fried Chicken and Waffles? C'mon, you know me better."

"I could have put it in a to go box…"

"You really wanted to cart that around with us today?" He sidestepped a family watching a mime unwrap an imaginary gift.

"Touché," she said.

They navigated over the uneven cobblestone streets that surrounded Jackson Square. People popped in front of them constantly. Many seemed to be young men dressed like Bart. Or was it that she was focusing on trying to catch a glimpse of him with his bimbo?

"I didn't think it would be this busy down here today," Rad mumbled.

"Me either." Carina paused at one of the street vendors. Their paintings hung from the wrought iron fence that surrounded the park. The scenes ranged from a rain-soaked kitten hugging a rat to a New Orleans lamppost twisted in a hurricane wind.

"Twenty-five percent off for Christmas," stated the haggard young man. He pulled his tattered jean jacket around him and stomped his feet for warmth. He wore a beard, which probably helped him keep warm.

Carina peered at the lamp post again and read the words aloud. *"Changes happen when you least expect it. In memory of those lost during Hurricane Katrina.* This is beautiful. I'll take it."

After the transaction was completed, Rad carried the picture. "Were you affected by the flood in Baton Rouge?"

"No," she sighed. "But my aunt's house flooded."

"What about your mom's?"

Pain slashed across her sweet face, and his heart froze. Her eyes watered. "No. She passed about two years ago in a car wreck."

"Oh, no. I'm so sorry. Your mom was such fun to be around." Rad felt bad for bringing it up, but there was no way he could have known.

"It's okay. I'm dealing." She swiped a tear from her eye. "Despite the fact that Bart was no support whatsoever during that time. Just that alone should have clued me in that we were no longer on the same page. But anyway…how about you? Did your house flood?"

"My apartment did. I was living in Denham Springs at the time. I woke up and stepped in water. Thought at first it was the plumbing but found out otherwise when I went onto my balcony and the entire parking lot was covered in water. Only the roofs of cars could be seen. It was so…otherworldly."

She placed a hand on his arm. "Oh, Radlykins, I'm so sorry."

He shrugged. "I didn't lose much. Had just moved in and only had a few things, so for that, I was fortunate. Lost my Jeep, though, and I had to move back in with my folks for a bit."

"So, they did not get water?"

"No, but it was rocky for a while. Their neighborhood became Islands Off O'Neal."

They both broke out in a rendition of Kenny Rogers and Dolly Parton's duet song, "Islands in the Stream." Linking his arm through hers, they paused in front of an artist who had honored the Cajun Navy with several paintings depicting their heroic efforts. During the 2016 Baton Rouge flood, local boat owners helped residents in East Baton Rouge Parish, Livingston Parish, and Ascension Parish escape from their flooded homes. The picture that caught Carina's eye depicted an airboat rescuing an elderly lady from her waterlogged front porch. She stood on the rail with her hand in her rescuer's as she stepped into a camouflage colored pirogue. In her arm was a tiny, wet puppy. Rad glanced at Carina, and when he saw a tiny tear slip out of her eye, he immediately bought the painting for her.

They walked into the park and took a seat on a cold metal bench. Carina shivered and pulled on her lower lip. "My aunt stayed with me. We got trapped too, so she couldn't make it back to her place for a few days. Of course, there was nothing we could do to the house anyway. No help. She's too old, and I am a pansy when it comes to physical labor."

"I'm so sorry. Is it any better now?" Rad set the painting on the bench between them.

A tear slipped down her cheek. "No. She's living with me. She had no flood insurance. FEMA gave her sixteen thousand, but how is that going to build a house that was worth three hundred thousand at one time? Her late husband had gambled away all their money, and when he died, all she had was the house and social security. She had just put it up on the market. So, she pretty much got the short end of the candy cane."

Rad's chest constricted. So many of his friends and family had lost their home the weekend of August 12, 2016. He had spent many days helping gut houses, and now he helped rebuild homes through his church. He took out his phone. "What's her name? Maybe I can put her on my church list of people in need."

Carina shook her head. "She's too proud. I had to put her on lists. My sister came down to help me clean out the house. It was a wreck. Aunt Rosalie had torn the place up looking for jewelry and cash that she had hidden everywhere. By the time we got in there, the mold…ew. It grew an inch if not more every day. I felt like I was in a science fiction movie."

"Rosalie what?"

"Simoneaux." She sighed and gave him her aunt's address.

A man holding a guitar stopped in front of them and broke out into song. Once he finished his rendition of "A Winter Wonderland," Rad stood, dropped two twenty-dollar bills in the open guitar case and requested a song in a low voice so Carina wouldn't here.

The man nodded and stretched his fingers by riffing on the guitar. Rad took a seat next to Carina, watching her out of the corner of his eye. He remembered a lot of things about her.

"Oh, the weather outside is frightful," sang the street musician. "But the fire is so delightful…"

Carina squealed and clapped her hands. After the guitar soloist finished and moved on, she smiled at Rad. "You remembered."

"Let It Snow" had been her absolute favorite Christmas song in high school. "How could I forget? We spent an entire weekend at your parents' camp listening to it over and over and over. So much for being goth."

"Yeah, our friends would have hated us had they known our hidden passion for Christmas."

"Guess we weren't meant to play on the dark side all the time." Rad casually placed his arm on the back of the bench. Carina snuggled into his embrace as they fell silent. They watched people passing by with kids or dogs or both. The sun warmed their faces despite the cool breeze playing across their skin. The sounds of the quarter echoed around them, and they became content in their companionable silence.

Until a shadow fell over them. Rad tensed, and Carina straightened up out of the crook of his embrace. She lifted her chin. "What do you want, Bart?"

Chapter 15

Jackson Square, French Quarter

New Orleans, LA

Sunday, December 25, 2016

4:30 PM

Carina

Carina tried to make her heart quit aching at the sight of her recently-made-ex-fiancé. Her right thumb automatically tried to rub the engagement ring. Of course, now that finger was void of its jewelry, as she had thrown it at Bart last night. The indentation remained in her flesh, and she moved her hands apart, even though they felt awkward just sitting in her lap.

With his upper lip lifted in obvious disbelief, Bart squinted at she and Rad. Her ex's head tilted to his right, and he blinked several times. Carina forced herself to stay right beside her old best friend. Her ex no longer had a say in what she did or whom she saw. She slid her hand into Rad's and lifted her chin.

"Well?" she asked. Her little heartbeat sounded like a toy soldier's drum, and her lungs caught her breath as if she had just stepped into a room void of oxygen. Deliberately, she inhaled as deep as possible and let it out with a controlled pace.

The sneer on Bart's face melted into a frown complete with a wrinkled brow and watery eyes. He dropped to his knees, bowed his head and held up an offering to Carina. In his upturned hands laid a black suede whip with horsetail ends.

Carina's mouth fell open as Rad stifled a laugh. She elbowed him in the ribs and forced herself to regain composure. She wanted to take the whip and shove it somewhere, but Bart might enjoy that. Instead, she sat back, folded her arms, and crossed her legs, swinging one so that he saw it from his submissive position.

"Not…on…your…life." Her words dug deep into her throat as she forced them past her lips. She bared her teeth as the struggle to control herself became next to impossible. "Get up. You're embarrassing yourself."

Bart lowered his hands, shifting so the whip was hidden. He lifted his head, and a single tear slid down his cheek as he took in Carina and Rad. "Is it him you want now? We can include him…"

Her eyes widened as she struggled to keep her mouth closed. Incredulity turned to rage that flared over her like flames in a fireplace. She jumped up, and as Bart was too close, he fell back on his butt in an attempt to get out of the way. "Wow. No. You…Ugh! I can't even begin to figure out what to scream at you right now. I am THAT ticked off."

"I can suggest a few words," Rad offered. The tone of his voice eluded to how much he was enjoying the show.

She glanced over her left shoulder just to confirm he wore the smug smile from his youth. She quickly looked back at her ex as hysteria threatened to overtake her. "Not helping, Rad."

Bart scuttled back. He took a deep breath, and his face morphed back to sneering. Getting back on his feet, he towered over Carina's five-foot five height. He adjusted his shoulders, dusted off his pants, and stuck the whip inside his coat. He lifted his chin. "So, this is it."

"I think it's been IT for quite a long time," Carina replied in a low voice. Her hands rested on her hips as she moved her head from side to side. "I'm just sorry it took me so long to see it."

A breeze blew over them, and Bart pulled the lapels of his overcoat close. "I'll leave your things in a box out back."

"Perfect." Carina crossed her arms and tapped her foot, anxious for him to be gone. Her blood boiled, effectively blocking any chill that may have overtaken her.

Mouth drawn into a thin line. Bart's glare shot daggers down at Rad. "Enjoy my sloppy seconds."

With a sweet smile, Rad stood and placed an arm around Carina's waist. His six-foot-one-inch frame towered over everyone. "Actually, I believe you have been enjoying mine."

Bart glared up at Rad, clearly trying to figure out what was meant. Stifling her mirth, Carina waved her fingers at him. "Bye-bye now."

Her ex straightened his shoulders, lifted his nose, and walked away. She watched him saunter until he was out of sight, just to make sure he was gone. Then and only then did she allow her shoulders to slump. Rad still held her and helped her sit down.

"Are you okay?" he asked, peering into her face.

Emotions bubbled inside, but the first to rise was laughter. She kept seeing the whip in Bart's extended hand. Disbelief quickly replaced the giggles, and she shook her head side to side. "Yeah. Actually, I am fine. He and I haven't been close in a long, long time. This is a side of him I never saw coming."

Rad sat back and surveyed Jackson Park. "I know what you need."

"A whip?"

They both laughed, and he stood, picked up both paintings, and held out his hand. She allowed him to lead her once again, and on the other side of the park, he moved his hand in a showcase wave. "Pick your carriage, m'lady."

Several mules and carriages lined the street, waiting on customers. A few people stood in front of each mule, but not the one Carina wanted. The minute she set on eyes on it, she knew it was the perfect buggy. She passed up the one cart that resembled Cinderella's, enjoying the look on Rad's face when she did so.

"I thought you always wanted to be a princess." His lips twisted like a pretzel.

"Yeah, you thought wrong." She climbed into the backseat of a red buggy with three rows of seats for multiple people. The mule pulling it had painted, red hooves, and the beast waited patiently for the orders to move. Carina held out her hands for the painting. "Give me that, and pay the man, my friend."

Chapter 16

The French Quarter

New Orleans, LA

Sunday, December 25, 2016

5:00 PM

Rad

Rad's right thigh pressed against the side of the mule-drawn buggy. He ensured there was as much space as normally possible between him and his old best friend. The lady had been through a lot in the past twenty-four hours, and he was determined to be a friend...not a rebound. So, he ignored the naughty thoughts that would keep him off Santa's nice list.

He snuck a peek at Carina. Her head was facing the left side, giving him a lovely profile in the light of the streetlamps. She swiped at her cheek, and his heart ached for her pain. He was certain if he could read her mind that she thought of Bart.

Where the heck she had met that guy and what she saw in the dude was beyond him. He could tell from the first moment that the guy was nothing but a spoiled, rich piece of coal that was used to getting his way.

The mule's hooves clomped against the cobblestone streets, and the buggy swayed gently as they made their way through the French Quarter. The large wooden wheels rolled over dips and potholes. Two older women sat on the bench in front of them. They spoke German, and Rad couldn't understand a word they said. He assumed they were tourists, and he recalled feeling relieved when they climbed on board. He had been fearful that a romantic couple would claim the seat, and he had not wanted Carina to be put in that position. He was certain all her thoughts spun around Bart now. She didn't need to be stuck with lovey turtle doves smooching in her face.

He tapped Carina's knee. The desire to caress her jean-clad leg overwhelmed him, but he slid his hand up and pointed his thumb behind him. "Look over here."

They had entered the Faubourg Marigny Neighborhood, which made a somewhat triangular shape from Esplanade to St. Claude Avenue to Franklin Avenue to N Peters St and back to Esplanade. The wide point of the triangle touched the bank of the Mississippi River. The buggy was at the corner of Esplanade Street and Royal. All the houses were lit up to honor the reason for the season. Even the trees in the median, the section that divided the streets into one-way passages, had decorative lights so bright that the streetlamps could have been turned off. White lights adorned one of the gingerbread-styled mansions. Elegance exuded from the home.

"I can picture ladies from long ago in their antebellum dresses sipping their mint-juleps on that porch," Carina said. The lights shone against her green eyes, and Rad blinked to remove the spell placed upon him by those eyes.

"And the men stank up the place with their lack of deodorant," he laughed. "Yeah, I'll take this time and age, thank you very much."

"Well, there was a paste trademarked in 1888 and called *Mum,*" advised the driver of the buggy. "So, while they did try various things for smelly sweat, I'm sure they weren't as good as modern technology."

"Interesting," Rad said. "I wasn't much of a history buff in school. The older I get, though…"

The rest of the ride, they listened as the driver gave various history lessons about the Faubourg Marigny Neighborhood, which had been established in the year 1805. It was one of the oldest neighborhood's in New Orleans, and it used to be a plantation owned by Bernard Xavier Phillipe de Marigny de Mandeville. He subdivided it and sold the lots.

While they didn't pass the house, the driver noted that the neighborhood housed the residence of Marie Laveau's father, Charles Laveaux at 1801 Dauphine street. Marie was the famous Voodoo Queen hairdresser who helped the poor of New Orleans by using a network of spies to acquire useful information. The lady's second husband, Christophe de Glapion, was a wealthy, white Creole who fathered seven children with her. Their cottage is located in the French Quarter on 1020 St. Ann Street, and the driver stressed that it was a must see for those who had never been to New Orleans.

When at last they returned to Jackson Square, Carina seemed to have withdrawn into herself. Rad helped her out of the carriage, and the touch of her warm hand sent sizzles down his arm. Her green eyes stared up at him in shock, and he realized she felt the connection as well.

He quickly released her and gathered up the paintings. "Hungry? Thirsty? In the mood for some karaoke at the Cat's Meow?"

Her eyes lit up. "Let's get some food and drinks, and then maybe some singing will follow."

"Sounds like a plan, but let's go put these in my room. I don't want them to get damaged."

After they dropped off the paintings, they entered the karaoke bar and found a table in the back. They ordered the H.O.T. line package which included seven drinks, a tray of Jello shots, a DVD of their performance, head of the line stage pass, and more. It wasn't long, and they were singing "Living La Vida Loca."

Three a.m. appeared too soon, and as the bar shut down, they stumbled out with the others, not quite sure of how time had passed so quickly. Somehow, they managed to find their hotel, and as Rad fumbled for the room key, Carina stared at the door to Bart's room. Before Rad could stop her, she pounded on the door, yelling her ex's name.

When a sleepy headed old man opened the door, her mouth fell open. She mumbled an apology and stumbled back to Rad with a candy cane red face. She grabbed his shirt and hung on as she got the giggles. Minutes later, they were both passed out in their respective beds.

Chapter 17

Magnolia Blooms Flower Shop

Baton Rouge, Louisiana

Wednesday, December 28, 2016

Noon

Carina

Peach juice dripped out of the basket, ruining everything inside. Carina grunted in aggravation. She knew she shouldn't have put the fruit on the bottom. She hadn't been thinking straight since she returned from New Orleans. Obviously, the breakup with Bart still dominated her every thought.

Dominatrix…

She shuddered at the thought of Bart's…kinky side. Not for her. No thanks. The only thing good that had come out of that trip was being reunited with Rad. He had definitely helped her get through one of the toughest days of her life. It ranked right up there with the day of the Baton Rouge flood back in August.

Sighing, she focused on the ruined order and pulled out the contents that were savable: a corkscrew, two wine glasses, and a bottle of champagne. The latter had to be wiped free of peach juice. The rest of the items— a white rose, the two mashed up peaches, and some squished grapes— were tossed in the trash along with the basket. She got them cheap, so it was no big deal.

After she redid the basket, she tucked in a new white rose between the glasses. White roses stood for new beginnings, purity, and innocence. As she wrapped the basket in pretty New Year's Eve cellophane paper, she wondered which of the three it stood for. She tied on a huge curly bow and picked up the card: *To the boy next door, here's to a New Year filled with promises! ~ Lily*

"Mystery solved," she whispered.

Carina's driver, Sam, was out on a run, and he had gotten a flat tire. She grabbed her keys and the basket and locked up shop to make this delivery. It was right down the road, so she wouldn't be long.

Seconds later, the basket was in the passenger seat of her old green truck, and she turned the key. The old engine rumbled to life, and Carina shifted it in drive and pulled out of the strip mall parking lot. She turned left onto Jones Creek Road, rolled under the green light at George O'Neal Road, and journeyed down to the other end of Jones Creek Road. She pulled into another strip mall and parked in front of a thrift shop called Southern Odds and Ends.

Her brain still full of disparaging relationship thoughts, she hauled herself out of the truck with the basket. The sidewalk in front of the store still had Christmas stuff out, but most were slashed to half off. Shifting the basket to one hand, she looked at the price tag for a metal, old-fashioned lamppost. The cut price was still more than she could afford. Shaking her head, she entered the store. The bells on the door jingled, and she yelped at the sight of the creature.

An eight-foot alligator stood on its hind legs right next to the entrance. Moss hung from its tooth-filled jaws, and blinking lights hung around its neck. A red Santa hat sat atop its head, and in its claws was a sign that read *Welcome*.

She blew out a laugh. This was something she expected to see in one of the smaller Louisiana cities…not Baton Rouge. *Where had the owner acquired this jewel?*

Thunder rolled around the store, and Carina glanced out the window as confusion set in. The sky was a little overcast but no rain. She perused the store, wondering why a clerk hadn't instantly appeared. She could have stolen all the stuff on the sidewalk and been long gone. She searched for the sound of thunder and found a machine at the checkout counter.

Setting the basket on the counter, Carina tapped the old, rusted desk bell. *Ting ting ting.* She played with the sound machine, making a mental note to put this on her shopping list.

"Carina?" the male voice asked from a direction to the right. A huge pile of artificial Christmas tree limbs covered a desk, hiding the person until he walked into view.

Her mouth dropped. "Rad? Is this your shop?"

He touched his nose with a smile. "Good detective work, Inspector Gadget."

She smiled. "Got my license from Cap'n Crunch."

He pointed at the basket. "How did you know where my shop was?"

"I didn't. Someone named Lily sent this to *the boy next door*. I assume that's you."

"Ah, yes." He nodded knowingly. "She owns the coffee shop a few doors down. She also rents one of the rooms in my house."

A flare of jealousy rose in Carina's chest. She squashed it like an ember from a sparkler. She wasn't Rad's girlfriend, so she had no right to such feelings.

"Well, looks like she is hoping for a spectacular New Year's Eve." Carina started backing toward the door. "Y'all have fun. Maybe we can get some coffee soon."

"Wait." He held up his hand. "Want to join us?"

She laughed and shook her head. "Didn't last week clue you in that I don't do kinky?"

His face turned candy cane red. "Oh…no…I didn't…Lily and I are going downtown to the watch the Red Stick drop on New Year's Eve. Besides, she and I are just friends."

Carina froze and a shade of pink crawled up her neck. "My bad. Yeah. Sure. Sounds like fun."

In 2013, Baton Rouge began a New Year's tradition entitled Red Stick Revelry. An LED-lighted Red Stick was dropped from the top of the Town Square Beacon. Festivities began around noon and lasted well into the next year with crowds dancing to live bands and partaking in various activities. She had never been.

"We are going to Uber, so I will text you the info," Rad said.

"Perfect," she said, still taking awkward steps back. She couldn't help but admire the handsome old friend before her. She pointed at him. "You have Christmas tree in your hair."

His brows furrowed as his hand reached up and grabbed the tiny sprig. "Thanks."

"No prob. See you soon, boy next door."

Chapter 18

Southern Odds and Ends

Baton Rouge, Louisiana

Wednesday, December 28, 2016

Noon

Rad watched Carina leave. He loved the way her hips sashayed. The movement was completely natural. She had no idea how provocative her walk was, but his body sure did. He shifted, trying to calm down.

The shop's bell jingled, and when the door closed upon her exit, he let go of the breath he had been holding. Closing his eyes, he willed his libido back into the cave.

He had heard Carina the minute she entered the store. Her tiny scream at the alligator had made him chuckle. He had been watching her on the camera system while she had looked at the lamppost for sale. The camera was set on motion detection, so it came to life when people were out front.

He felt a tad guilty for covertly watching her as she came up to the counter, but New Year's bells, she was a looker. In high school, she had been pretty. As a woman, she was a knockout. The dark circles under her eyes ticked him off. He was certain those came from crying over that sack of coal who didn't deserve her. Rad was glad she had found the man's true colors. For all Bart's flashy gold, he was nothing but a user.

Sighing, Rad went back to putting up the tree. He didn't want to be Rebound Rad, but damn if he didn't find his old best friend attractive. They had slipped back into the comradery of years ago, and his old crush on her had flared to life with even more gusto. A little weight fell on his shoulders as he reminded himself that now was not the time.

Patience is a virtue…tell that to my…

He shook his head and tried to focus on something else. The shop was too quiet even with the sound machine, so he turned it off in favor of a local radio station. Country music filled the silence, and he sang while piddling around the shop.

The bells on the door rang as someone entered the store. Rad sat at his desk, playing solitaire on the computer. His heart dropped at the sight of his ex. Mina was with her brother, Earl, and they rushed up to the counter.

Rad picked up the box behind his desk and carried it to them. She was looking at the gift basket, reading the card. He pushed the box in front of her and moved the basket to the floor.

"Here's your stuff. Have a nice life," he growled away the tiny ache in his heart.

"Who's Lily?" she asked with her nose in the air. Her dark brown hair fell in waves down her back.

"My new girl." Rad stepped as far from the counter as possible.

"Hmm, that didn't take you long."

"How is *your* new girl?" he stared into her eyes, daring her to deny the relationship.

Mina leaned forward, smacking her lips. "She tastes like cotton candy."

Earl grabbed the box. "C'mon, sis. Don't be that bitch."

"Why not?" Rad asked. "It certainly suits her."

She simply stared at him. He saw a mixture of emotions play through her face and eyes, but he was tired of her manipulating ways. He pointedly looked at her brother.

"How's it going, bro?" Rad held out his hand.

The guy smiled and accepted the handshake. "Going great. Plant work is tough but pays the bills. How was your Christmas?"

"It was good. Spent it in New Orleans with some buddies. Don't remember much about it," he laughed. "Well, except for the girl..."

He didn't bother to mention which girl. He wanted his ex to squirm, and she did. He still refused to look at her. "One-night stands...love 'em and leave 'em."

"What about Lily?" his ex asked with a smirk.

Oops...

"We have an open relationship," he replied and wiggled his eyebrows. "Not that it's any of your concern anymore."

She lifted her chin and narrowed her brows. Her catty smile didn't reach her eyes. "Oh, I certainly don't care who or what you do. We've been done for a long time, *bro*. It just took you a long time to realize it. Have an awesome New Year."

"Oh, you can bet your sweet candy cane I will," Rad replied. "I have plenty of girls lined up...all ripe for the taking."

Rolling her eyes, Mina turned on her heel and stormed out, not even waiting for Earl. The ice in the room left with her, and the two men stood awkwardly while the radio started playing "Your Cheating Heart." That broke the tension, and both men laughed.

"Well, I guess I better go. See ya around," Earl said as he followed in her trail.

"Later," Rad said. He shook his head, scratched his chin, and went back to playing solitaire.

That's another piece of coal that I am glad to be rid of.

His thoughts turned back to Carina, and he found himself looking forward to New Year's Eve for the first time. It felt strange to be excited about something rather than dreading it. He hadn't been too crazy about going to New Orleans. He had fought his buddies about going, but now he was more than pleased with his decision to go. Had he not gone, Santa wouldn't have delivered his Christmas gift. And what a gift it was…one high school crush at the perfect time.

Chapter 19

Lily's Car

Baton Rouge, La

December 31, 2016

5:00 pm

The windshield wipers swooshed back and forth, dancing with the rain that splattered on Lily's car. Carina sat in the backseat and stared absently at her phone, not really looking at the screen. Her fingers played with the ring-style popup on the back of the phone. Rad sat in the passenger seat as his roommate, Lily, drove.

The rain had Carina even more depressed. She'd been looking forward to the evening all week, but now melancholy covered her like wet mud. Thoughts of the happy times with Bart had been slamming at her all day, but then so did the unhappy memories.

Taking a deep breath, she tried to focus on the song blaring from the radio. The country music told her that blue looked good on the moon but not in her eyes.

Too bad, Keith Urban, I am sticking with my green eyes.

"Hey," Rad looked at her over his left shoulder. "Since it's raining, we were thinking about going to a party. The house is downtown, so we can still see the fireworks."

Carina nodded, pushing down anxiety at the thought of mingling with strangers. "Sounds good."

"They better have food," Lily stated as she turned the car onto Millerville Road. "I haven't eaten since breakfast."

100

Rad's roommate wasn't a knockout but was very pretty. Her friendly, almost too bubbly personality took over as she rattled on and on about this and that. Carina tried to pay attention but had to fight to keep her brain off Bart. Secretly, she thought Lily talked too much.

Ten minutes later, Lily parked the car on North Fifth Street by the State Capitol Park. It had taken a while to find the spot, and they trekked through the rain down Spanish Town Road to North Seventh Street, where the party house was. Carina questioned her decision to go out, pretty much deciding the night was already a flop. At least she had thought to bring her raincoat. Rad held an umbrella over Lily's head, but it wasn't big enough for three people. When they arrived at the house, Carina's tennis shoes were soaked. She considered calling an Uber, but one pleading look from Rad changed her mind.

Surprisingly, the night went by fast. Conversation flowed. She found she had much in common with Rad's friends, a far cry from the snotty people Bart associated with. Somehow, she managed to do a good job of forgetting about her ex. Every time his name popped in her head, she struck up a conversation with whomever she stood next to.

By the time 11:30 arrived, the small shotgun house was wall-to-wall with people. Rad and Lily found her chatting with a dude that rattled on and on about racecars. Grateful to see her friends, she excused herself.

"Thank you for the save," she whispered to Rad as he grabbed her hand.

"Your resting Scrooge face gave it all away," he laughed.

"I am not, nor will I ever be, a racecar girl." Carina followed Rad as Lily pushed their tiny train through the crowd to the tiny back yard.

The rain had slowed to a drizzle, so they stayed on the covered back porch. There were a few other people with them as they waited for the fireworks. The back of the house faced the Mississippi River, so they anticipated a great view despite the rain.

Carina sipped from a fresh bottle of beer. She had a great buzz going and was glad Lily was the designated driver. She could have gotten really toasted but did not want a huge hangover. So, she had stuck to beer.

"Hey ..." Rad started to say something but paused.

The moment she met his eyes, the world slowed to a heartbeat, and old high school feelings drifted to the surface. She had fought the attraction back then, not wanting to lose her best friend. The same held true now.

She put her fingers to his lips, slowly shaking her head. Her lips wanted to taste his with a desire that rivaled resisting a fresh, hot, chocolate cake. "We cannot go there."

The porch light glowed upon his face, and he simply stared at her. She wondered what he was thinking behind those puppy dog eyes, and her heart hurt. She wanted desperately to throw caution to the wind.

People around them began counting down, but they remained locked in some crazy tug of war. Well, Carina knew *she* felt the battle between friendship and love. She had no clue what was going on behind those warm brown eyes, but his pupils were dilated, so she knew he desired her...or someone.

"Well if you won't kiss her..." said a deep, southern, male voice. A warm body pressed against her right shoulder, and body chemistry instantly meshed. Carina turned her head to the right just as a bearded face swooped in and captured her lips. The clock struck midnight, and the New Year rang in with fireworks over the river and over her lips.

Her eyes fluttered as she inhaled the oceanic scent of a man's cologne, and she snuck a peek at Rad. He stared at her with desire, jealousy, and remorse, but Lily threw her arms around him, planting her lips against Rad's.

Ah what the Scrooge...time to live a bit vicariously.

Carina closed her eyes and turned toward the man. She wrapped her arms around Mr. Beard's neck and let herself get carried away by the stranger's New Year and new-her kiss.

Chapter 20

Spanish Town Parade

Baton Rouge, LA

Saturday, February 25, 2017

9:00 am

Mardi Gras in Louisiana is just as big as Christmas. It's also known as Fat Tuesday, as the state holiday always lands on the Tuesday before Lent begins. The weekend and Monday before host many parades throughout the state, and Baton Rouge's Spanish Town parade has rolled ever since 1981. It's the city's most controversial parade, with past and present floats including political and lewd themes.

Carina held onto the side rail of the float. The pickup truck pulled them down College Drive as they headed toward the parade startup. Rad stood next to her, dressed in a pink and white striped, old time, Victorian style, men's bathing suit that looked more like a romper. He even had a matching straw hat and had tinted his beard pink. A pink flamingo floatie wearing a chain of beer bottles sat around his waist. The float theme was *Stay Afloat* and coordinated with the parade's theme *Come Hell or High Water, It's Slippery When Wet*. The theme basically thumbed its nose at the infamous 2016 Great Flood of Baton Rouge.

Her outfit matched Rad's except in a woman's old Victorian bathing suit. Her cap had ruffles on it, and she held a pink parasol with tiny beer bottles attached to the edge. Her ruffled bloomers were knee length, and the matching socks went to her knee. She had chosen white tennis shoes because she knew that walking around in heels was out of the question.

"Thanks for taking Jerome's place," she said loudly. The cool wind from the ride whipped over her face, causing a piece of hair to get stuck in her mouth. She pulled the strand out and tucked it over her ear. The sunny day warmed her chilled skin, but she still wished she had brought a light sweater to thwart the sixty-five degree temperature.

Rad smiled, showing a set of perfect, white teeth. "You're welcome. I've never ridden on a float before. Been to plenty of parades. So I'm pretty psyched about this."

She grinned and wiggled her eyebrows. "Get ready to be addicted. You get to peg people with beads and get away with it. Laissez les bons temps rouler!"

A lady on her left handed her two shot glasses filled with an amber colored liquid. "Let's get those good times rolling now, Carina."

She raised an eyebrow, accepted the drinks and handed one to Rad. They tapped the shots together. "Bottoms up."

The icy sting of alcohol slid down Carina's throat, and she winced but sucked up the momentary discomfort. "So how is Lily?"

Rad's cheeks turned pink, and she wondered if it was from the alcohol or subject matter. He grinned like a schoolboy but wiggled his eyebrows like a horny teenager. "I never knew my roomie knew such...wonderful tricks. That tongue of her's..."

Carina held her hand up. "Too soon, bro, too soon. I'm glad y'all hooked up."

Liar.

That one word bounced around the slush pile of her brain. She kicked the thought and jealous feeling away.

"Speaking of...how's that new boyfriend of yours?" Rad asked as he pulled a beer out of the cooler and handed it to her.

"It's okay. He's so busy with work that I don't see him much through the week. Although he has brought me lunch once or twice."

"Hmmm," Rad wrinkled his mouth. "Sounds like some other joker you recently kicked to the curb. You sure you want another so-called workaholic?"

She twisted her lips and leaned on the rail. Some cars honked as they passed the float, and fellow parade riders threw beads at the vehicles.

"No. Definitely no," she said and swigged some beer. "But I don't want anything too serious right now anyway. I wanna play that field."

She laughed because she knew she wasn't much of a player. "So, what made you decide to ask Lily to be your girl?"

"Oh, it's not like that." Rad waved his beer bottle around. "We aren't exclusive. At least, I'm not."

Carina nodded. "FWBs. Gotcha. Hope she realizes that."

Rad's brows furrowed as he thought on it for a second. "Yeah...me too."

Several hours later, they were having the time of their lives throwing beads into the crowd.

Bend...grab from the bead box...pick a target...ping— got 'em.

All the while, everyone danced to the tunes played by the float's DJ. The music ranged from eighties hits to modern day rap. Sadly, it was over much too soon.

Rad swapped hats with Carina as their float passed the last of the crowd. He tucked his hands under his chin and batted his lashes at her. "Why, Rhett, Rhett, whatever shall I do without you?"

She stuck her nose in the air. "Frankly, my dear…you know I don't give a damn…"

He placed his hand over his brow and threw his head back. "Whatever shall I do…"

"Drink your damn beer, and dance, my friend, dance," Carina chanted as the DJ cranked up more party tunes.

Thirty minutes later, they were back at the rendezvous point where they had loaded up. After helping clean up the float, they got to Carina's green truck and sat on the tailgate. Carina felt exhausted and still a tad tipsy. "I'm not so sure either of us needs to drive right now."

"I already called us an Uber."

"You want me to leave my fine truck here in some random parking lot on College Drive?" Carina's eyes widened in mock horror. Truth be told, she was certain nobody would mess with it. Carefully, she laid back in the truck bed and stared up at the blue sky. "I had a blast today. Reminded me of the good ole days in high school."

"Remember when we went to that drama festival, and the school gave us detention the following week because they *claimed* we didn't have permission?" Rad tapped his fingers against the side of the truck.

Carina rolled her eyes. "Oh yeah...but we had such an awesome time. What scene did we do? I can't remember."

"You were Maggie the Cat. I was Brick." Rad leaned over her. "'What is the victory of a cat on a hot tin roof?'"

Sitting up, she smiled at the memory. "Why...'Just staying on it, I guess...'" Carina breathed in her sexiest kitten voice. "'As long as she can.'"

Carina blew him a kiss like Elizabeth Taylor did to Paul Newman in the movie. Rad's face hovered just a few inches from hers, and the desire to find out how his lips tasted drew her closer. Just before she did so, she stopped herself. Her eyes met his heavenly blue ones, and she fought their pull by forcing herself to look down.

The tiny sound of meows reached her ears. "Is that..."

"Sounds like kittens."

They both climbed out of the truck and searched around for the source of the sounds. Rad lifted the lid of a dumpster, and his shoulders slumped. "Well, at least it's empty..."

Next thing she knew, he was inside the trash bin and handing her a tiny newborn kitten. "Is the mother in there?"

He sighed. "Yes, but I don't think you want to see her. She won't be joining her babies. She's dead."

"Aw," Carina said, cradling the kitten. "How many are left?"

"Only this little fella," he said and handed it to her. "Two out of five..."

Carina's heart tugged at the thought of the dead mother and other babies. "I hope the Uber doesn't mind..."

"If he does, then we'll call another." Rad hopped out and landed beside her. His dapper bathing suit was smudged with garbage stains. He took the tan colored kitten. "One for you, and one for me."

Carina held up her black-colored one. "Maggie."

"And Brick," Rad held his up. "Hopefully, their names match their genders because I am clueless when it comes to that sort of thing."

They went back to the truck, and as they waited on the tailgate for their ride, Carina watched Rad cuddle the kitten. She had forgotten about his love for animals, something Bart did not share. She had yet to find out how Jerome felt about them. She loved animals, and the fact that Rad did too...well, that made that attraction to him just that much harder to resist.

Chapter 21

Valentine's Day Delivery

Baton Rouge, La

Tuesday, February 14, 2017

6:30 PM

Carina struggled with the basketball-shaped vase as she climbed the set of stairs. She sighed in aggravation and blew a leaf out of her face. The bouquet consisted of anything other than roses. Obviously, the recipient was a guy. Well, that's what she assumed as all she had was the first initial and an address. It could be a woman who loved basketball for all she knew.

Of course, it's on the fourth floor, and of course, there isn't an elevator.

The sun had set, and the stairwell wasn't well lit. Carina's pepper spray was in her pocket. *A lot of good it will do me there…*

Her hands were wrapped around the cold vase. If someone tried anything, she figured she'd just lob the heavy thing at them and run like one of Santa's reindeer. She imagined the scene, including seeing her clumsy self, tripping on her own two feet. *I'd be doomed.*

At long last, she made it to the fourth floor and paused to let her breath catch up. She'd left that on the second floor, so it took a minute. Meanwhile, she surveyed her surroundings.

The apartment complex must have been adults only. She hadn't seen any kids and still didn't. She was a tad grateful for that as she didn't relish the thought of dodging playing children while balancing the very expensive and heavy delivery.

110

Apartment 412…

Carina had memorized the number since she couldn't risk fumbling with the card nestled in the massive bouquet. Today had been grueling, and everyone in her shop had assisted with deliveries. This was the last one and as it had been on her way home…

After finding the apartment, she kicked the door with her foot, hoping it sounded like a knock instead of the dull thump of a shoe. The floral tucked into the basketball vase blocked her vision and tickled her nose. When the door swung open, she couldn't tell who it was.

"Delivery for G."

"Holy cupid's arrows. You're late delivering these," growled the woman as she took the vase from Carina. "Why?"

"Um…Valentine's Day is always busy," Carina said and stood awkwardly in the doorway. She tried not to sound snippy as she was exhausted.

The woman had already turned her back on her, but Carina still heard the woman's short snort and mumbled words of *no tip for you*. Most people didn't tip anyway, so she didn't expect it.

"Carina?" whispered a male voice to her left.

Turning her head toward the direction of the stairwell, her gaze fell upon the man who had kissed her on New Year's Eve: Mr. Beard. They had been dating ever since, but she hadn't known where he lived. Her face lit up.

"Hey, Jerome. I didn't know you lived in this complex."

As he approached, she waited for a kiss, but he sidestepped her and entered the apartment, acting like he didn't know her. "Honey, I'm home."

Carina's jaw dropped as her heart fell like a petal off a dying flower. She felt the blood drain from her face as her eyes rapidly blinked. Slowly, she pivoted toward the door, disbelief fogging her brain. *Not again…*

The woman returned to the door, but Jerome still stood in the entrance, blocking Carina's view. His six foot three, muscular body did a fabulous job of it, too. He was a workout nut.

"Here. Give this to her even though she's late and doesn't deserve a tip," snapped the female.

Jerome obliged, and as he handed the money to Carina, she saw the wedding band on his finger. The cad obviously removed it when they were together. Her heart hardened as she snatched the tip out of his hand.

"Well," she growled. Her lips pulled into a frown. "Guess this is goodbye."

His eyes held a touch of sadness. "Yep."

She leaned in close. "Lose my number," she whispered.

Frowning, Jerome simply nodded and shut the door. Carina stared at the white wood, wanting to scream and kick it down. His wife didn't…well, maybe the snooty bitch did deserve it.

But not with me…

Her heart ached from the virtual knife lodged in it. *How do I keep getting myself into these situations? Do I have a neon sign painted on my forehead that only creeps can see?*

Her leg vibrated with the desire to kick at his door. A few cracked eggs would look lovely against the brown paint as would a few strands of toilet paper. Sugar in his tank would work too.

Pushing away the juvenile thoughts, Carina stomped back to her car, infuriated beyond belief. She hesitated as she spied his truck. Her hand held tightly to her keys as she imagined dragging the tip down the side of the red vehicle. *Loser* would look nice on his driver door, and *sucker* would be appropriate for the passenger side. Both she and his wife fit that word to a T.

Carina forced herself to get in her car. Shoving the keys in the ignition, she turned up the radio volume and screamed as loud as she could.

Such a fool…why can't I find a decent man? An honest man? A single man?

Tears slipped from her eyes, and she swiped at them. They wouldn't stop, and she dug in the glove box for tissue.

Don't break down in his parking lot. Gotta get out of here.

As she sat up, she looked into the face of the man who just broke her heart. Stealing herself, she lifted her chin and her middle finger.

"Can we talk?" he asked.

"Go to hell." She threw the car in reverse and headed to her best friend's house.

Hopefully I ran over his foot…

Chapter 22

Rad's Apartment

Baton Rouge, La

Tuesday, February 14, 2017

7:15 PM

Rad set the vase of red roses on the coffee table, smiling as he heard the soft jazz drifting from Lily's bedroom. They had become more than roommates, and he considered her his girlfriend even though they hadn't made it official. He planned on changing that tonight.

Popping open the bottle of wine, he pulled down two glasses and poured in the liquid gold. He set them on a silver tray and arranged chocolate-covered strawberries around. All the while, he imagined her waiting for him under the covers in her birthday suit. Balancing the tray in his left hand, he made his way to her door.

Rad knocked briefly before pushing open the door. He stopped dead in his tracks. The sight before him was completely unexpected.

Lily sat on the floor with her bare back to him. She was naked as a jay bird, and her hair lay enticingly against her skin, swinging slightly as she rocked from side to side. She sang hauntingly in a low hum.

Well, that was completely expected...

In front of her was a tiny cauldron atop of a camping stove. The scent of butane filled Rad's nose as his jaw dropped. His roommate muttered strange words and swayed while waving leaves

114

over the cauldron. Green and red smoke swirled up from the bubbling pot.

She's a witch?

Rad didn't believe in the supernatural, but living in Louisiana had taught him a lot. There were plenty of residents who did, and superstitions ran deep. However, in the back of his mind, he always believed this sort of stuff only happened in New Orleans and other outlying parishes— not Baton Rouge.

"What are you doing?" he growled. His voice sounded foreign and loud.

Lily jumped, twisting her body to look at him. Surprise shone in her eyes as she struggled to get up. "Crud. I meant to lock that door. What time is it? You're early."

"Yeah, I closed shop early to spend the night with you." He pointed at the cauldron. "Please tell me that's chicken soup."

She glanced at the liquid before pinching the bridge of her nose between her fingers to alleviate a sudden headache. "Well…there is a chicken leg in there, so…"

Rad left the room, brought the tray back to the kitchen, and practically threw it in the sink. His Christian upbringing warred with the idea that witchcraft was being done under his roof. It pissed him off to no end, and he paced the living room, waiting for Lily to come out.

A few minutes later, she did. She had donned a robe and instantly tried to cuddle up to him with a hug. Her touch sent chills over him, but he couldn't tell at this point whether they were from revulsion or fake desire. He gently pushed her away from him.

"So, what kind of spell were *attempting* to do? Because you know all of that crap is a bunch of hocus pocus," he snapped.

Lily lifted her chin and crossed her arms. "Oh, don't be so sure of that. You seem to have fallen for me pretty hard."

His mouth fell open as he stared at her. Speculations whirled in his brain along with the crazy dreams he had been having. "A love potion?"

Leaning her back against the counter, she inspected her fingers and shrugged. "More like a friends-with-benefits potion. I just wanted a bed buddy...not your heart."

Rad narrowed his eyes, and his mouth tightened. *So, this is how it feels to be used...* "Get out."

"But—" Her shoulders sagged as she pushed away from the counter. Her bottom lip pushed out prettily, and she gave him puppy dog eyes. "Can we have one more romp?"

Wow... Forcing himself to look away, Rad moved to the other side of the kitchen and pointed to the door, ignoring her request despite the flare of libido. "You need to leave now. I know you have someplace to go. You can come get your stuff later. I'll gladly give you back this month's rent in full. Just...go."

Her mouth fell open as she stared at him. With a tiny huff, she stomped her foot and rolled her eyes. "Drama King."

As she got dressed and put together a few things, he sat on the couch and fumed. No, he did not believe in spells, but nonetheless, how could he trust that his feelings for Lily were real? Not that it mattered because apparently, she just wanted him for his bedside manner.

Most guys only want that anyway…but not me. I want to settle down.

She stepped out of her room, suitcase in hand and several bags on each shoulder. She shifted awkwardly from one foot to the other. "No hard feelings?"

He blinked slowly and quirked his left eyebrow. "Could I trust them if I did?"

She tossed her hair out of her eyes. "Well since you don't *believe*…then it shouldn't be a problem."

He rose. "I don't. What I do believe is that you played on my budding feelings for you. Had you just let it develop on its own …"

She rolled her eyes. "Please. I never intended this to last. I just wanted to ravish your fabulous bod."

Rad was certain other guys wouldn't have blinked twice at that confession, however, he sort of felt exploited. *So, this is what it feels like to be used…*

"Well, you got what you wanted. Don't let the door hit you on your broomstick." He strode to the door and pulled it open. Carina stood with her hand raised to knock. He drew up at the unexpected visit. "Oh, hey."

Her eyes looked past him. "Am I interrupting something?"

"Nope. Lily was just leaving."

Chapter 23

Rad's house

Baton Rouge, LA

June 22, 2017

7:00 PM

Rad stood on the porch of his house, and the wooden slats pressed against his bare feet. The sun was going down behind his home, and the evening gave way to a tiny smudge of relief from the heat. The Louisiana humidity, however, pressed on. His forehead beaded with sweat, and he wiped it away with the back of his hand.

Carina waved from her car. The sun reached over the roof of his house and shone brightly on her face, highlighting the sparkles in her eye shadow. She rarely got dolled up. "See you tomorrow, right? Dinner at my house?"

A long sigh escaped his lips. He desperately wanted to run down the steps, over the pointy rocks that made up his walkway, and drag her away from the car like a caveman laying claim to a cavewoman. Instead, he pasted on a smile and turned his right thumb up. "Absolutely. I'll bring the Moscow mules."

Sliding into her vehicle, she left to go on yet another date. She had stopped by his house to bring him leftovers and had only stayed a few seconds. Since Christmas, they had returned to Baton Rouge and resumed their friendship. On one level, it felt like they had returned to their high school friendship. He pined for her while she continued to see over his head. However, he still refused to make a move to get her to see him in a different light. The timing was off. He would not be Rebound Rad.

But the more they hung out as *friends*, the more it became apparent that he had fallen back in love with her. And the more it seemed she picked the wrong guys to date. How was he going to open her eyes so that she would see him as more than just a friend? How long would he need to wait to make a move? Was it supposed to be forever, or did it just feel like it?

His left hand clung to the container of lasagna, and he lifted it to his nose. The plastic couldn't contain the wonderful aroma, and once her car drove out of sight, he went inside, shut the door, and plopped on the couch. He dove into the food, not caring that it wasn't on his diet. Tonight would be a cheat night.

The television lights flickered as an infomercial promoted their upcoming Christmas-in-July sale, and currently featured a cd of holiday songs. The next song that blasted through his living room was "Let It Snow" by Frank Sinatra.

"Ah, torture," he growled.

Carina's favorite song. Why did everything remind him of her? The day they had reunited had been magical for him, even if she viewed him as a friend. He cherished the memory of waking up in the same hotel room with her as well as those of walking on the levy in the dying sunlight.

Stop it.

He flipped the channel to sports, picked up his phone, and googled *how to get her romantically interested*. He scrolled through a few stupid suggestions before clicking on one that offered help on

119

getting a female friend to make the first move. The first was to make oneself available.

Ha. Been there, doing that.

The website suggested setting up "an accidental romantic situation" and to "drop hints." Well, duh, Wiki-How. He had been doing that. Heck, he had started that on Christmas Day.

Too soon.

Maybe it was time to lay it on thick. He needed to figure out a way to make her look at him as boyfriend material. How to do that without making her run away?

Like when you were eighteen...

She had slammed the door in his face after kicking him for smashing her cell phone. His teenage-self had fumbled that up right well.

His eyes lit on a painting hanging above the fireplace. Carina had given it to him. It was one of the ones they had bought together in the French Quarter of a New Orleans lamppost twisted in a hurricane wind. He had read the words beneath the lamppost a million times. *"Changes happen when you least expect it. In memory of those lost during Hurricane Katrina."*

"I'm waiting," he sang to his furniture. Unlike the animated fixtures in *Beauty and The Beast,* the candles on his mantle refused to come to life and offer up answers. He and Carina had just watched the movie the other night...at her request, of course.

Frustrated, he looked at his watch: 7:30 pm. Still time to catch up with his friends at the sports bar down the street. His friend Pete had texted him earlier, so he knew where they were. If he drank one beer when he got there, he'd be okay to drive after a couple hours.

But what if she comes back? Her dates never go as planned, and maybe I need to wait for—

Turning off the tv, his hand hovered over his cell phone. His fingers curled inward, and he forced himself to leave it on the end table.

Maybe it's time to be less accessible…

He grabbed his keys and headed out into the warm summer night.

Time to be distracted…and maybe find a female to be attracted to…one who notices me…

But somehow, he didn't think he'd find someone whom *he* would notice.

Chapter 24

Rad's house - front porch

Baton Rouge, LA

June 22, 2017

11:00 PM

Carina sat in the dark on Rad's porch. Yet another date from Hell. Why did she continue to pick all the wrong guys? What was wrong with her? Would she ever learn her lesson and find Mr. Right?

Tonight's fiasco included paying her own way, receiving the wrong meal because her date had insisted that he knew French, and watching him play video games on his phone for the better part of the evening. The final straw had been ending up at the movies to see a cartoon. Granted, she would have loved doing that with Rad, but not on a first date.

Impressions, people. Impressions.

While she knew her date was younger, she didn't realize how much younger until he'd pulled out his Velcro *Star Wars* wallet.

Teach me to pick up a nice-looking man dressed in a business suit in a comic bookstore. Just because he reads Buffy the Vampire Slayer comics does not make him dating material.

Carina sat back in the rocking chair, playing with the edge of the Styrofoam food container. She planned on throwing the escargot— slimy snails— away as soon as she could. Where was Rad anyway?

She glanced at her watch: 11:00 pm. Stifling a yawn, she closed her eyes, praying he was safe wherever he was. For some reason, she didn't feel like going home yet. She had so much to tell him about her Gameboy date. Texting wouldn't suffice. She had tried calling, but he hadn't answered.

Carina closed her eyes. She had been blessed to get his friendship back last Christmas. God had given her a much-needed gift. They spent a lot of time hanging out, watching tv, laughing, and cutting up like when they were kids. She had gotten back her best friend, and despite the dreams she'd been having about him, she intended to keep it that way. She couldn't stand the thought of losing his friendship.

Her dreams, however, kept giving her pause. All included Rad in his Christmas boxers, climbing into her bed like a tiger seeking to devour her; popping up from the other end of a huge bathtub filled with bubbles; and even one with him holding that black, suede whip.

Taking a deep breath, she forced herself to think of white clouds floating in blue skies. She pictured a fishing rod in her hand and a soft, warm breeze caressing her skin. Wind sang through the tops of trees as brim fish popped the top of the water and ate bugs. A fly landed on her cheek, and she swatted it away. Several more appeared as the sky suddenly became dark. She slapped at the flies, but her hand connected with a face. The slap wasn't hard and did nothing to stop what happened next.

Soft lips captured hers, and the scent of the man kneeling before her enveloped her senses. Despite the darkness of the porch, she instantly knew it was Rad from his woodsy cologne. The situation seemed too surrealistic, so Carina figured it was part of the dream and gave in to the kiss.

She wrapped her arms around his neck, inhaling more of his scent that triggered a tingling rush through her blood. Her fingers played with his hair. She loved the way the buzz cut felt under her fingertips. The kiss felt right on so many levels, like coming home to a batch of freshly baked cookies. His taste of caramel warmed her to her toes.

If only life could be like this dream, Carina wished as she kissed him back with unrestrained passion, thinking she still dreamed. *So why not give into my deepest desire…*

Rad's warm hands cupped her cheeks, and she kept her eyes closed as the kiss ended. His lips pulled away as if molasses kept them together. He rubbed his cheek against hers, and the stubble dug into her skin. Her eyes popped open as realization hit her.

Definitely not a dream!

A heartbeat later, Rad pulled back and stumbled to his feet. "Oh…I shouldn't have done that. I'm sorry. You just looked like an angel sleeping on my porch."

Carina blinked. It wasn't a dream. Her hand went to her mouth, and she just stared at him. Why hadn't she seen this before? Her heart jumped as she recognized the emotion.

When did I…could it be…love?

He took her silence the wrong way and cursed. "Sorry…shouldn't have taken those shot…"

Ah, that made more sense to her now. He'd been out drinking, which explained the missing presence of his truck. "Who brought you home?"

"Pete's girl...designated driver." Rad swayed and flung his hand out to catch his balance. He missed the post, stumbled back, and fell down the stairs.

Carina jumped up, and the container flew out of her lap and spilled open on the porch. She was at his side in seconds. "Rad! Are you okay?"

He laid on his back on the sidewalk, looking up at the stars and clearly stunned. "Well, that was dumb."

"Can you move? You didn't break anything did you?" She placed her hands on his left arm, which rested on his stomach.

Rad carefully moved his legs and arms, testing them. His right hand went to the back of his head. "My head hurts."

"You need to go to the emergency room." She helped him sit up. The light from the lamppost lit the area well, and she glanced at the back of his head. "It's not bleeding."

"No ER," he slurred.

"You might have a concussion."

He tilted his head and winked at her. "Then keep me awake with your sweet southern kisses."

Carina should have been aggravated with him, but she was more grateful that he appeared to be okay. She met his blue eyes as realization told her brain what her heart already knew. "You were right in front of me the whole time."

"Didn't mean to let that happen...the kiss, that is. Sorry." He looked down at his lap. "Shoulda left ya sleeping."

"That's not what I meant." She slid her fingers under his chin and forced him to look at her. She pressed her lips to his and explored the possibilities. Everything crashed in on her. They'd become closer over the past six months. Spent so much time together that little fights were mended almost immediately. That they had history made it so much sweeter.

When the kiss ended, she stared into his eyes. "I see you now."

Chapter 25

Rad's house - front porch

Baton Rouge, LA

June 23, 2017

1:00 AM

The angel looking down at Rad uttered words he never thought he'd hear. His heart filled to the point it might explode, unfortunately matching the throbbing in his head. He ignored the pain as his eyes teared up. His masculine pride warned him to suck it up, but his drunkenness batted the thought aside.

"You're better than an angel," he whispered. "Cuz you are flesh 'n blood…'n here…w' me."

Carina slid her hand in his and helped him sit up. "ER time, bud. You are gibbering."

He waved his hand. "No, I'm fine. Better 'n that. I'm in love with my best friend…who sees me now …"

He paused as his eyebrows furrowed. "Or…did ya mean something…less…um…"

Idiot, too soon. His stomach flipped, causing all the alcohol to churn like a volcano, ready to explode. He closed his eyes, fighting nausea and embarrassment.

She pressed her fingers over his mouth. "It means…I love you."

Eyes flying open, Rad released the breath he'd been holding. His shoulders dropped, and he smiled. "Whew. I was scared I'd said the *L* word prematurely."

She smiled as she helped him to his feet. "Took me long enough to figure it out."

He swayed and grabbed her hand for support. "An' then ya do it when I'm drunk."

He narrowed his eyes. "If yer hoping I'll ferget..." He waved his index finger side to side. Or tried anyway. It ended up on her lips, and their softness distracted him. He wiggled her lips until she laughed. His hand slid under her chin, and he focused on aiming for her mouth. When his made contact, the kiss exploded with unspoken words.

Thoughts and emotions pummeled Rad's fogged brain. He pulled away, intent on declaring a few of them. It felt like he was grasping at butterflies. "Still sorry about yer phone."

Carina shook her head. "Over it."

A sudden pounding encompassed his head, and closing his eyes, he pinched his nose and bent down to his knees. Nausea filled his mouth, and he seemed to sober up instantly. Carina knelt beside him, hand on his shoulder.

"Rad? What's wrong?" Her voice was laced with concern that warmed his heart.

"Um, yeah, I think my head hit the ground pretty hard."

"Let me grab my purse. We're ER bound."

Her feet echoed on the steps as she ran up and then back down to him. Her purse swung on her shoulder. He had managed to stand back up, feeling an ounce better. The back of his head throbbed with the beat of his heart. "Okay, but can we get a burger on the way?"

She smiled, nodded her head and grabbed his hand. Leading him to the car, she mumbled, "Can't keep a man's stomach empty."

Pulling her to a stop under the streetlight, he tugged her close. "My stomach maybe empty, but my heart's full of you."

Epilogue

Rad's house

Baton Rouge, LA

Dec 24, 2017

5:00 PM

Carina kicked the door shut behind her, balancing bags on each arm. Where was Rad to help her? She'd been calling and texting but no response. He had stayed home cooking while she ran some last-minute errands. The crowds were atrocious, and she regretted waiting this long to finish Christmas shopping.

She had moved into his place a few months ago, letting her aunt stay at her place rent free. The stress of the flood had taken its toll on the woman, and while her aunt's house was almost ready to put back on the market, it would never get the price of what it once was worth. Carina didn't mind helping her aunt, though. Family takes care of one another.

She set the bags down and went into the living room, stopping at the sight of a present in front of the Christmas tree. The box was the size of a refrigerator and wrapped with the comic sections of the newspaper. A huge, green bow was wrapped around the box with a tag on it.

Please open now before I suffocate.

Carina laughed, and with a shake of her head, she yanked off the bow and tore away the paper, which fluttered to the floor around her. "Copycat."

She pulled open the cutout door, but instead of finding Rad in his Christmas boxers, she found an assortment of cell phones from flip style to androids. A flower arrangement laid in the center of the phones. The bouquet consisted of daffodils. They symbolized new beginnings, and she smiled at the memory of teaching Rad the different meanings of flowers.

Nestled on top of the bouquet sat a gray box the size of a deck of cards. Carina's heart flip-flopped, and with shaking hands, she picked up the box and flipped open the lid. A diamond the size of a pea sparkled. Her mouth fell open as masculine hands slipped around her waist from behind.

"I'm so grateful you made that Christmas mistake last year," Rad whispered in her ear. "Will you marry me?"

The heat of his body enveloped her. She twisted around with a smile and touched her finger to his nose. Without answering, she indicated for him to stay put as she slid out of his arms and picked up her phone. A few seconds later, she set the phone down. Her hips rocked side to side as instrumental music filled the room. The karaoke version whispered around them, and she began to sing the lyrics to a popular Christmas song.

"This Christmas, I give you my heart, and I promise next year, I'll be here to stay. This year, you saved me from tears. I promise the answer is yes."

Thank you for reading *The Christmas Mistake*!

Please consider leaving a review. Reviews help

readers find their next favorite book.

If you liked this book, you may also enjoy these GenZ Publishing Romance titles:

Going Home for Christmas by E.A. Stripling

Take My Whole Life Too by Justine Ruff

All You Hold On To by K.T. Egan

Made in the USA
Monee, IL
28 December 2020

55476308R00083